SULTRY NIGHTS

A JINN'S SEDUCTION

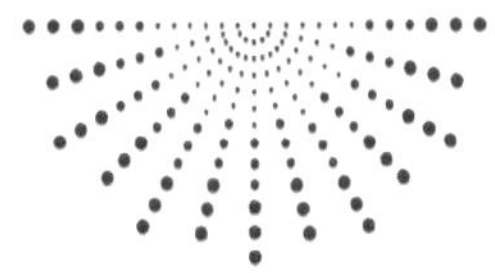

VALERIE TWOMBLY

Sultry Nights

❀ Created with Vellum

PROLOGUE

*C*rone gazed through heavy lidded eyes at his master as he sucked the meat off a chicken carcass, as if it were his last meal. From time to time, he'd toss a scrap at his beloved Irish setter and laugh while looking at Crone, who was forced to sit at the old warlock's feet. Crone vowed from the first day of his servitude, he would kill the bastard. Yes, Morden was old, and he was powerful, but Crone was confident he would one day succeed.

"Are you hungry," Morden asked, laughing hysterically. "You're a Jinn, certainly you can conjure your own meal."

Crone fisted his hands and clamped his jaw tight. The only words that would escape his mouth would no doubt get him beat, or worse; the warlock could refuse him the time to see to his brother's needs.

Morden jerked on the chain attached to the mystical silver band around Crone's neck. "Answer me!" the warlock demanded.

"Fuck you," Crone snarled. So much for keeping his mouth shut. He'd been at the bastard's beck and call for three years and he'd had enough. "Do your worst."

Morden smiled. "Oh, I intend to. You may be my best assassin, but you still lack manners. I will have your respect."

Crone didn't stop the laughter that bubbled to the surface. "You fat

"

fucker. One must earn respect, and you can't get that from torturing a man. The only thing you'll ever earn from me is a blade shoved into your black heart."

The warlock leaned as far forward as his fat belly would allow. "You should know that you cannot kill me, and your threats will only earn you pain."

Crone snorted. "I'm numb to your beatings." He'd had his flesh stripped from his body, his eyes gouged out, his chest ripped open, and his beating heart pulled from its resting place and laid before him. He'd been forced to drink a vile concoction that caused his gut to burn, and the vomiting episodes had been like swallowing fire in reverse. The worst, though, was his inability to shift. Morden's magic choker held Crone in his human form. Unable to shift to smoke put Crone on edge. Jinns needed to shift like they needed to breathe and got pissy when they were unable. Usually they worked off their steam with a good fuck, but that had been taken away from him as well. Morden found great amusement in displaying his sexual exploits in front of Crone, who had sported a raging hard on for far too long.

That too made for a pissy Jinn.

"You might be able to bear my pain, but I will finally break you. I've waited for that moment since I first tricked you into becoming my assassin."

Morden liked to take credit for Crone's predicament. However, it was the love for his brother Armand that caused his current state of affairs. The bitch genie, Cyndel had cursed his brother to live as a powerless immortal in the human realm below them. Armand built a decent life in Spain with Crone's help, but when Cyndel finally tired of Crone's many threats, she'd shut him out. He had been the only family member allowed to visit and assist Armand. When she banned Crone, he'd done something he never thought he would. Begged on his hands and knees to be allowed back into Spain. After much thought, Cyndel agreed with one condition.

Crone becomes indentured to Morden.

Crone's past victim swept through his mind. Once his master placed the death mark on his prey, and Crone was ordered to murder, there was no stopping him. His mind may still be very much coherent, but free will was gone, and his body only obeyed Morden. After the first couple of kills, Crone learned how to mentally shut down. He'd distance himself from his prey, and with the precision of a well-oiled machine, he'd carry out his master's wishes. It didn't matter the age or sex of the victim. If Morden commanded the death of a woman or child, Crone must obey. There was one comfort, however; Crone held control over how he killed his victims.

The young warlocks were dealt with as swiftly and painlessly as possible. The older men... Many of them, warriors and often warlocks, wished to prove their magic was stronger; hence, a bloody battle would ensue. It was the only time Crone was allowed to use his Jinn magic, and he had gained a reputation. Crone, the son of Efrain, middle brother to Armand and Lazaro, was a force to be reckoned with. He wasn't proud of the fact his name caused terror among so many immortals, but one thing was certain. He would gain his freedom one day, and Morden would die by his hand.

He flashed Morden a lazy gaze. "Give it your best shot."

"I will do precisely that." The warlock snapped his greasy fingers and several of his slaves appeared, taking away empty dishes and wiping down the table. When they'd finished, two others dragged in a struggling female. She too wore a silver collar around her neck, indicating her magic was suppressed. Most likely a witch and definitely not here of her own free will.

"I'm in the mood for some entertainment," Morden announced, pushing his chair back and standing.

Crone stiffened but said nothing. Things never went well when the warlock was bored and a female brought in tied as this one was; it usually meant Morden would rape her and make Crone watch. He schooled his features while his insides burned with fury, and he thought of ways in which to torture the warlock once he freed himself.

Morden moved to his cushioned armchair across the room, while his slaves pushed the dining table against a wall and rolled out several furs onto the marble floor. The lights dimmed to a soft glow, and someone released Crones chains. Not a good sign.

"Beautiful, isn't she?" Morden asked with a slight chuckle in his voice.

"You're a disgusting pig. Why don't you for once pretend you're a decent immortal, and let the girl go."

The warlock's mouth twitched. "Tell you what. I am a reasonable man and to prove it, I'll let you fight for her life." He snapped his fingers. "Bring the girl to me."

Crone shot a glance at the witch whose black robe was yanked from her body, leaving her nude. A pretty girl with creamy skin, full breasts, and straight black hair that fell to her rounded hips. She definitely would cause a stir among the men. Morden's minions shoved the girl and forced her to kneel on the furs at the warlock's feet.

"Now. Fight the Sataric and win then I'll free the female. Fail? She dies."

Crone cringed. The Sataric, a beast of Morden's own making, had a human body with the head of a bull and stood seven feet tall. This battle could go on for some time. Of course, he could refuse and let the woman die. After all, she meant nothing to him, but her pleading gaze bore straight to his soul. For once, he could save a life rather than take it.

"Bring on the beast and give me my power," Crone demanded.

Morden snapped his fingers, and a rack of weapons materialized next to where the warlock sat. "No magic, but you may chose a weapon from this rack."

Crone snarled as he walked over and made his selection. He picked up a battle-ax with leather strips that crisscrossed a dark wood handle, giving an excellent grip. It was long enough for a good swing. He flexed his biceps and wielded the instrument, delighted with the way it moved and how the bat shape blade's edges cut through the air.

"I'll take this one."

Morden nodded. "Wise choice." He waved to his minions. "Send in the Sataric."

Crone knelt next to the girl. "What is your name?"

"Tara," she whispered.

"Don't fear, Tara. I have every intention of winning." He jumped to his feet as the beast entered through the gate. "You are an ugly fuck." He braced himself for attack.

Seven feet of pure angry beast charged him. Crone shifted to the right, out of harm's way. One thing was certain, these were dumb creatures and predictable. He'd fought them before and won so was confident he'd claim victory this time. All he needed to do was be patient and stay out of the way of the enormous horns. Eventually the beast would tire. Again, the Sataric lowered its head and charged, but this time Crone was too slow. A horn caught him in the side and tossed him like a rag doll. Pain shot through him, and he hit the ground and rolled, losing his weapon. Blood poured from the open wound.

"Now that just pissed me off." He pushed to his feet as the beast turned to make another run. Crone spotted his battle-ax in the center of the room. He made a split-second decision to run for it, dropping to his knees as he slid across the floor. Scooping the ax up, he leaped to his feet seconds before the beast was on him.

He swung.

The blade made contact just above the Sataric's knee, taking his leg clean off. The creature dropped with a blood-curdling scream. Crone needed to hurry and finish or the beast would grow another limb. Before Morden or his minions could interfere, he wielded his weapon and sent the head rolling across the floor, leaving a trail of blood in its wake.

Crone threw down his weapon, ignoring his pain and the open wound. He marched toward Morden and Tara. "I beat your piece of shit pet, now let her go."

Morden rose. "That was too fast."

"Really? You should have picked a more fitting challenge. Face it, I'm the best fucking assassin you've ever had."

"Today you will learn your place." Morden grabbed Tara's hair and jerked her to her feet, but she showed no pain or fear. Her nakedness obviously didn't bother her, as she stood tall ready to accept whatever fate handed her. "I'll free the witch." He produced a dagger and before Crone could react, he planted it deep in her chest.

"You son of a bitch!" Crone shouted and dropped next to Tara, whose blood now stained the fur.

"I freed her of her miserable existence. She should be thankful to you for that." Morden and his slaves vanished, leaving Crone alone with Tara.

He pulled her head into his lap. "I'm so sorry." His stomach flipped as he realized he'd done this. He might as well have held the blade himself and shoved it into her gut. Images played through his mind of the many ways he was going to torture the warlock. "I swear to you here and now. When I am free, I will avenge you. He will pay for what he has done."

She looked at him, her eyes clouding. "I-I believe you are a man of your word." She coughed blood, and he gently wiped it away. "My family... Protect." A rattled breath. "May my ancestors watch over you." She drew her last breath, and he watched the life vacate her brown eyes.

"May your ancestors guide you home." He kissed her forehead and vowed revenge would be his.

CHAPTER ONE

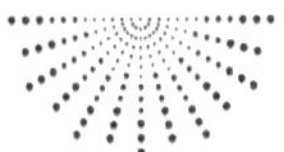

urrent Times:

Crone fought to keep the irritation from showing on his face, lest his brother, Armand, kick his ass from here into the next kingdom. While he loved his new sister-in-law Kayla, he wasn't one who liked taking orders. Granted, she was now the queen of Eral, but it still rubbed him raw that Armand assigned him the duty of the new queen's advisor. He was a warrior, not a babysitter.

"Hello?" A faint voice penetrated his fog of boredom.

"Yes?" He stared at Kayla.

"You didn't hear a word I said." She wrinkled her nose in annoyance.

He batted his lashes. "Of course I did."

She folded her hands and placed them on the table in front of her. "Okay, answer my question."

Shit, busted. He sighed. "Fine. Yes, I was tuning you out but not intentionally. You know I love you, but I hate politics."

She smiled. "I know you'd rather swim in a pool of piranhas, but I think you'll enjoy this." She waved a folder under his nose. "This woman needs a protector, and she asked for you personally." Kayla leaned forward, laying a manila folder on the desk. "She's paying in gold *and* she's pretty."

He straightened in his seat. Intrigued, he reached for the file. "A protector, you say?"

"I knew that might grab your attention. Tessa is a witch who apparently is being pursued by a demanding warlock."

His body stiffened at the mention of a witch, and his memories flew back to Tara. After she'd taken her last breath, he stayed with her. Holding her cold body until the guards had finally come to haul her away. It was after they'd pried her from his grip that he'd gone completely mad. They'd forgotten about the weapon that now lay on the floor several feet away. Somehow he managed enough power to summon it to him. In the blink of an eye, he'd decapitated both guards. Unsure if it was sheer determination or the gods smiling down on him, he managed to find Morden unaware. He held to his promise and killed Morden, but not before he'd dissected the warlock piece by piece. His death had been slow and painful. With every cut from his dull blade, he'd uttered, "This is for Tara." He'd managed to keep the bastard alive and suffering for months, until he finally grew bored with the torture and finished him off. He'd thought of her often, and had even gone in search of any living family but had run into a dead-end.

"Crone? You've wandered off again."

He focused back on his sister-in-law and the present. "I don't wish for the job. You can give it to another."

She blinked. Of course, she didn't know what happened to him. Only his father and Lazaro knew about his past. Not even Armand was privy, since he'd been banished to a small village in Spain, and Crone had been sure to never mention it while on his visits. He'd pulled extra duty and performed more than one kill to buy temporary freedom for those visits to his brother the first few years he'd been banished to Spain. It had been worth it.

"I don't understand. A beautiful woman. Gold. Why would you

turn it down?" She studied him as if he were under a microscope. Kayla was an excellent observer, and he squirmed beneath her observation.

"Do I need a reason other than I have things to do?"

"There's more than you're telling me so either spill or take the job. You were asked for specifically, and she's willing to pay a lot for your services."

He let out a slow breath and picked up the folder, flicking it open. Inside was a photo of a woman with long, straight black hair and brown eyes that looked at him as if searching for something. He had to swallow a gasp because he could swear that Tara was about to leap off the paper right at him. He quickly flipped to the next page where an absurd figure had been scrawled on it. The amount of gold she was willing to pay for his protection... Something didn't add up.

"I'll take it," he stated.

Kayla smiled. "Good. I'll contact her and get the particulars."

Tessa stared at the newspaper until the words became a black and white blur. She still couldn't believe she'd gotten canned. Hilda, the owner of the small Wicca shop in town had shaken her head in disbelief and told her she needed to stop casting spells. She was a disaster in the making and when she'd summoned a demon by mistake, she'd been sent packing. As of right now, she couldn't afford to pay her rent without the income from the little store, and the part-time job she held at the bar was also teetering on the edge.

She dropped her forehead on the wooden table. "Ugh. I'm such a damn klutz." Her boss at O'Leary's pub told her if she spilled another drink on a customer, she was toast. Her life was one miserable mistake after another. She was always short on cash because she couldn't keep a job. Her clumsiness affected her finances and dating life. With her shy nature and plain-jane looks, the simple fact was that even if she did get a date, she'd more than likely end up wearing her dinner down the front of her blouse.

With a heavy sigh, she picked up her head. "What a sad state of affairs. I'm twenty-five and still a damn virgin. I wonder if being a spinster is back in fashion." The paper wasn't going to do her a bit of good. There were no jobs, and if she didn't come up with a plan quick, she would end up sleeping on the street. She looked across the room, and her gaze landed on the thick book that stood on the cheap plastic shelf. Chewing her lip, she recalled her earlier inquiry to the new Jinn queen, Makayla. She'd hastily asked for Crone to become her guard and made a promise she was unable to keep. Sure, she still possessed the one bar of gold that her mother had handed down to her, and maybe he would accept it as a down payment, but it was a far cry from the fifty bars she'd promised. However, if her plan worked then hopefully it wouldn't matter. She'd take back what belonged to her and become a strong witch. But if she failed...

"What if the tales aren't true?" she whispered to no one. The tattoo on her back tingled to assure her that they were——or at least the part about being bound to a warlock. Zadicus had already shown himself. Announcing he was the descendant of Morden, he gave her until next month to get her affairs in order before he came for her.

With a sigh, Tessa jumped from her chair and plodded to the bookcase. Pulling the old leather bound book from its resting place, she went to the kitchen and started the kettle for a cup of tea. Placing the book on the counter, she pulled out a stool and plopped down on its torn seat. The gold embossed emblem on the black leather, the same symbols that matched the tattoo on her back, stared up at her. She traced her fingers along its raised edges, a tribal crescent moon with a red star that hung from its upper tip. The mark every woman in her family carried somewhere on their body. Hers was on the back of her right shoulder and, as she recently learned, alerted her when Zadicus was close.

She flipped open the book and went straight to the middle. Even though she'd read it a thousand times, she wanted to make sure nothing had been missed.

Every witch from the Blackwood line, who is born on a Harvest moon, shall gain special powers. These powers will only be unleashed when said witch loses her virginity. The witch must be careful, as her lover may also take the power from her, if he is stronger in magic.

The kettle whistled so Tessa got up from her seat and shut the burner off. She pulled a bag of chamomile from the canister, dropped it into a stained mug, and poured the steaming water over the top before placing the kettle back on the stove. As she passed the counter, she scooped up the book in one arm and headed to the couch, where she settled in and flipped back to her page.

If a witch should lose her power, another virgin in her line may try to gain it back. If this is accomplished, said witch will become a most powerful Elemental: a witch who is one with nature. The Elemental witch may also break the spell that was cast long ago, bonding the Blackwood witches and the Demois warlocks.

Tessa took a sip of tea and swallowed; the warm liquid helped to settle her nerves. She flipped to the back of the book where a folded piece of paper sat tucked between the pages. Her heart pounded every time she pulled the note out and read it. The words never changed. They told the brief story about how a Jinn named Crone had fought a beast to save her grandmother's life. Even though he succeeded, the warlock still shoved a dagger into her chest. Her Nana had been a strong witch. Somehow, even after Morden took her virginity and her power then handed her off to one of his minions for breeding, she still had something left. Apparently, she'd handed off the last of her magic to Crone, while she'd also called upon the ancestors and requested that one of the Blackwood witches become the Jinn's *vetemba*. A match that was both powerful and rare. Tessa had only heard of one other time a Jinn and witch had been joined. In this case, Crone's female happened to be Tessa. The story had been told to her by her mother when she was only a child. Tessa's mother had pleaded with her, when she'd given her the block of gold, to find Crone and fulfill her destiny. Allowing the Jinn to take her virginity would not only give her the chance to gain Nana's power back, but the ability to end the curse. Logic said it was a good match.

"Shit. Who am I fooling? If this Crone is the same one who has Grandma Tara's power, I'm basically jumping from one forced bond to another." The thought of sleeping with a stranger left her cold, but if she didn't do something, Zadicus would be back to make his rightful claim. What choice did she have? Both her grandmother and her mother were claimed, and later killed, by the Demois family. She would be next, and her daughter, and on down the line. It needed to end, and it had to end with her.

She closed the book and took a deep breath. Somehow, she would have to outsmart a Jinn, not let on that she was really his chosen, get Nana's power, and break the curse so she could finally be free. "Get in, get out. Piece of cake." Right. Maybe for an ordinary witch, but she failed at everything she attempted.

She glanced at the clock; the Jinn queen should be calling her...

Her cell phone screamed an Adele tune. Not wanting to seem anxious, she let it go for several seconds before answering.

"Hello?"

It was the Jinn queen. "Yes. You have my address, correct?" She waited while the woman on the other end rattled off her apartment number. "Good. I'll be ready and waiting. Thank you." Pushing the end button, she tossed her phone on the coffee table and jumped up. Biting her nails, she paced back and forth.

"Ok, so he agreed." Great, it's what she wanted, so why had fear unsheathed its claws and ripped into her chest? She went back to the folder, sitting on the kitchen counter, and flipped it open. The picture she'd managed to find of Crone stared back at her. Bright blue eyes framed by black hair, and a well manicured goatee. A gold hoop adorned each ear; the man looked like he'd just stepped off a pirate ship. She couldn't help but wonder that if his picture stirred a fire deep in her sex, what would the man do to her in person?

"Likely feed me to the lions." She would have to spend the last of her savings to get a makeover. Maybe she'd stand a slight chance of seducing him.

❀

Crone took the folder with him after Kayla phoned Tessa the witch and made arrangements for them to meet. He was to go to her apartment in New Orleans tomorrow afternoon. He had to admit, he was curious how this female was connected to Tara. He'd know soon enough. Once he was brought up to speed on what exactly he was expected to do, he could figure out a plan. Taking on a pissed warlock wasn't his idea of fun times, but he owed Tara. Morden had used her to punish him. He still woke up everyday and apologized for letting her die.

Lazaro waltzed into the room as if he owned the place. Crone loved his little brother, but sometimes his sibling had more attitude than Crone himself, and that was saying a lot.

"Do you ever think to knock?" he questioned.

"Why?" Lazaro stopped. "You gotta girl in here?"

"If I had, you would have scared her off."

Lazaro gave him a wave of dismissal. "Nonsense. You're only worried I would have stolen her from you."

"As if you could," Crone commented as he got up and walked to the glass-topped bar where he poured himself a brandy. Swirling, he inhaled before taking a taste.

"What? I gotta pour my own?" Lazaro planted himself on a leather-padded stool and stared at his brother.

Crone pushed the crystal decanter in front of his young rival along with a glass. "I'm not your damn *criado*."

His brother rolled his eyes and grabbed the brandy. "You wouldn't know how to be a servant, but maybe you could learn some manners."

"Did you come here to insult me?"

"No, but it does lighten the mood." Lazaro flashed a devilish grin. "I really came to ask what the fuck you're thinking?"

Crone stroked his goatee. "At the moment? I'm thinking it's been a while since I've been between a wench's thighs, and I need to rectify that pronto."

Lazaro sipped. "That's not what I meant."

Crone's eyebrows rose. "Spit it out for fuck sake."

His brother studied him for a moment. "Why are you taking this job for the witch?"

Crone set his glass on the bar top. "Why does our sister-in-law find it necessary to blab?" he growled.

"She mentioned it in passing and since she has no idea about your history, she wasn't being a gossip. So, back to my question."

Pouring another drink, Crone contemplated if he should come clean or not. However, having someone to bounce this off of might prove useful. For all their small squabbles, Lazaro understood him. "I refused at first...until I saw the photo. I swear Tara was looking back at me." He rubbed the rim of his glass.

"You think she's a relative?"

"I searched the entire planet for her family and found none, but I'm thinking this girl has to be a descendant."

"I see. You obviously still carry guilt."

He raked his fingers through his hair. "Fuck! Of course I do. You've no idea what the ordeal was like."

Lazaro leaned closer and placed his hand on Crone's arm. "No, I don't know your agony, but I do know the kind of man you are. One who holds honor and loyalty above everything else. You fought to save her but in the end, it wasn't up to you."

Crone shook his head. "It was my fault." He squeezed the glass until it shattered in his hand. Blood trickled onto the bar top and mingled with the brandy. "I still should have been able to stop Morden." He clenched his jaw so hard it ached.

"You got your retribution when you finally took his life."

He watched the blood drop to the tile and memories of Tara, her own blood covering his body, flashed through his mind. "It wasn't enough. She mentioned family, and I think she was trying to tell me to protect them. If this Tessa is related then I owe her."

Lazaro sighed. "I know I can't talk you out of this, so if you need help, I'm here for you."

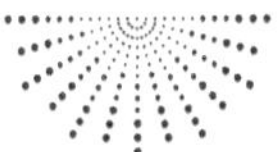

essa stared in the mirror and blinked several times. With a new cut and style, and now makeup, she hardly recognized herself. However, it definitely suited her..

"You are smokin' hot," the girl helping her commented.

"Thanks. I'll take all of it." She could smell the melting plastic from her credit card and still had to buy a few new outfits.

Once she'd checked out, she headed down the street to a small boutique she'd walked past every day on her way to and from her job at the Wicca shop. Many times, she'd stop in the morning while the small store was still closed and stare in the window. Envisioning herself wearing the outfit displayed on the mannequins, she would dream of having an ordinary life and a hot boyfriend. She certainly could never afford such nice clothes, and fear of her incompetent magic kept her from conjuring her own. As far as the boyfriend, her curse made being near a man impossible. However, since she was in dire need of help, she decided to wander in and see if the shop girls would be able to assist her in finding something to fit the bill.

"Hi, my name's Mandy, how can I help you today?" a cheery young blonde inquired.

Tessa felt her confidence bump up a notch. "I need something sexy but not overboard." She shifted her weight. "It's a blind date, so I don't want to come across as...you know, too much."

The girl nodded. "I know exactly what you mean." She walked to a rack of dresses. "Is this evening or daytime?"

"Umm, late afternoon."

Mandy grabbed a couple of dresses. One in bottleneck green, another a cobalt blue, and one in a vibrant berry. "Follow me and I'll put you in a dressing room. We'll start with these and see how you like them. You have such a lovely skin tone." The sales girl opened a room and hung the garments on a hook. "I think a low heel, maybe even a pretty sandal. Let me go look while you change." She sauntered off and left Tessa alone with the dresses.

She tried on the green and immediately pulled it back off. The color wasn't her favorite. Next came the blue. As she stood looking at herself in the mirror, she came to one conclusion. *I had no idea I had this much cleavage.* She wanted to seduce him, but this left her feeling like the girls would make an appearance any moment. Last came the berry. She adored the color and when she slipped it on, it was instant love. The richness of the hue against her skin was perfect. The deep scoop of the neckline showed the slight swell at the top of her breasts, yet didn't leave her worrying about falling out. The rest of the dress clung to her curves, and even she was impressed.

A knock came. "Come out and let's see."

She swung open the door and stepped out.

"Oh wow, that looks very nice. Here, try these." Mandy handed over a pair of black sandals.

Tessa moved to sit on a plush stool and pulled on the shoes. With a low heel, a wide strap across the top of her foot and another thick strap around her ankle, they were sexy yet functional. She walked to the mirror to view the complete look.

"Ohh, I love this."

"It shows off your assets nicely," Mandy complimented.

"I'll take it. Now, how about some jeans and a couple of tops."

"You head back into the dressing room, and I'll bring you some things to try."

By the time Tessa left the store, she'd purchased the dress, two pairs of jeans, a couple of tank tops, and two pairs of shoes. Her card was close to being maxed and her nerves strung tight. She glanced at her watch. Two hours until he would arrive at her apartment. Just enough time to get home and change.

Crone strode down a narrow hall and stopped at the door marked with the number three. He wrinkled his nose at the dingy carpet beneath his feet The building was a pig pen, and if this Tessa was by some slim chance Tara's family, he would remove her from the premises posthaste. No blood of hers should live in such squalor. He did have to wonder why she would choose to inhabit such an establishment. Was it possible she was giving up her life savings to hire him?

He squared his shoulders and knocked on the door. Light footsteps, undetectable to a human's ear, came closer. Finally, the door swung open, and he nearly took a step back.

Shit!

She'd been pretty in the photo, but the woman who currently occupied the space on the other side sizzled with sex appeal.

"Hi, you must be Crone?" her voice carried soft and sexy.

"I am."

She stepped aside. "Come in."

He moved through the doorway and into a small living room. Doing a quick scan of the area told him a lot about her. She was neat and liked things in order. Not a speck of dust touched the room's surface. A thick, leather-bound book stood out among the others on the case. Most likely, her ancestors spell book. He turned to focus on her. Her dress molded itself to her skin, and he tried hard not to notice the swell of her breasts.

Double shit.

"So, who are you exactly?" he asked, never one to beat around the bush.

She took a step back. "I told Makayla who I was. Did she not provide you with the information?"

"Yes. However, I need to know *everything* about you if I'm to provide protection."

"Oh. As you may have guessed, my grandmother was Tara. You remember her?"

He'd never forget. "I remember."

Sadness crossed her face. "I never got to meet her. My mother told me the story of what happened and how you tried to protect her."

He furrowed his brows. "I searched for any remaining family and found none. How did your mother know what transpired?"

"My mother was there and witnessed the entire thing."

Crone nearly retched. The daughter had watched her mother die? He wanted to kill Morden all over again. "What do you mean she was the there?"

Tessa steeled her shoulders. "My mother was eight at the time. Morden kept her hidden from you but made her watch. It was his warning of what happens when you defy him or his family."

"Son of a bitch." Disgust and hatred filled him. "I'm so sorry I failed. Had I known Tara had a daughter, I would have torn the place apart until I found her." Was that what she'd been trying to tell him? He'd failed at that as well.

"You couldn't have known, nor could you realize Morden intended her death all along. She'd defied him the entire nine years he held her captive." She shook her head. "I'm sorry. My manners are lacking. Please have a seat." She gestured toward the furniture in the center of the small room. "Would you like something to drink? Tea? Coffee? I might even have a beer in the fridge."

"No, but thank you," he stated sitting in a chair. "Please tell me more."

She took a seat on the couch. Her dress hiked slightly to reveal long legs, and Crone imagined them wrapped around his waist. *Damn. What the hell is wrong with me?*

"My mother was handed over to Morden's son."

Crone stroked his goatee. "I'd no idea he had a son."

Her brown eyes filled with hatred. "Yes. He handed her off to another warlock family to be raised. When she turned twenty-five, he claimed her just as his father had claimed my Nana. I was born and raised with the family then allowed to leave when I turned eighteen."

"Why do they allow you to leave then come for you later?" He was having trouble making sense of this.

"It's another form of cruelty. Allow us to enter society and get a taste of freedom so they can later snatch it away from us."

"I see, and where is your mother now?" He feared her reply.

"Dead."

Tessa focused on the man who sat across from her, his blue eyes piercing her soul. She thought she'd been prepared for the Jinn named Crone, but when she'd opened the door... If sex could walk, it had sprouted legs, waltzed right into her living room, and sat in the chair across from her. Why did she ever think she was any match for this man? Power, carnal energy, and the scent of black leather mingled in the air and sent a spark of sexual tension that lashed out and landed smack between her thighs.

He raised a brow and promptly furrowed it. "I am sorry for your loss. Can you tell me how the women in your family came to such a fate?"

"They were cursed several centuries ago by an ancient warlock." She rubbed an invisible spot on the hem of her dress, hating the fact she had to give him ammunition he might possibly use against her later. However, she had to trust him...a little. After all, he had tried to protect her Nana.

"The first female in my family to be taken was generations back. She was marked with the warlock's symbol on her body, which is passed to all the Blackwood women in my family. A curse comes with the marking that makes us easy to locate. Around our twenty-fifth birthday, a descendent of the original warlock comes to claim his Blackwood witch. They take our power, and then choose the man who will father our next daughter so the cycle continues." She intentionally left out how the warlock took their power. That was something he absolutely did not need to know. Too many questions would be asked.

Did he realize Nana had given him her power? Or the fact his mate currently sat across from him? The witch she'd purchased the blocking spell from had assured her that the Jinn would not be able to detect she was his *vetemba*. Tessa wasn't positive how it kept Crone from knowing, but she would do anything to remain hidden. At least until she decided what to do about the mating.

He studied her as if searching for the truth. Was he capable of seeing through her and discovering all of her secrets? After a long pause, he asked, "So this warlock you wish to be protected from, I assume, is one of the Demois descendants?"

"Yes." She tamped down the fear that he would suddenly change his mind. The man could win a poker game hands down. His features, not even his eyes, gave away anything.

"What are you *not* telling me?"

Crap. Had he figured out already what she was? She understood there was a chance he would eventually realize she was his *vetemba*, so she fell back on something a friend had taught her long ago. Deny, deny, deny. "I don't know what you mean."

His left black brow arched high over a pool of blue, and he looked at her as if she were a child who'd been caught with her hand in the cookie jar. "One thing you need to learn. I'm not a man with much patience. How does the warlock take your power? Is that what Morden did with Tara?"

Quick, think! "Yes, he took her power, but I'm not positive how." She plastered on the best poker face she could muster. Let him believe her Nana had no power when he'd fought to save her. The less he knew, the better for her. He scrutinized her, but settled back into his chair and seemed to ponder her words.

"Okay. This is what I propose. I can take you to a secure location where you'll be safe, while I research more on these Demois warlocks. If you are agreeable, pack what you need and we can be on our way."

She hadn't expected the bit about leaving her home, but again she wasn't sure what she expected. Perhaps he'd hang out in her tiny apartment and watch over her? Yeah, that was a stupid idea. Besides, soon she'd get kicked out for not paying her rent, and then what? She'd have to explain she was dirt poor, and he'd not be getting all the gold she promised. *Stupid! I could just tell him the truth and hope he agrees to hand Nana's power over to me while we have sex.* Suddenly, it dawned on her... *What if he has a wife?* One thing she did know about the Jinn. They were devoted to their loved ones, and no matter how much she tried, there would be no seducing him. Was it even possible for him to marry if he had a *vetemba?* She wasn't sure.

Panic mingled with the acid in her stomach and rolled around. "Do I need to worry about a jealous lover? Wife?"

His mouth curved into the most delicious grin. "You've nothing to fear on that front. I'm between lovers, and a wife is not even on my radar." His gaze dropped to her breasts, and her nipples hardened as if on command. "Are you offering?"

"No." What the hell did she mean no? She should have said yes and been on her way to getting exactly what she wanted. Apparently, the Jinn had her rattled.

"That's good, because I don't believe in mixing business with pleasure. Clouds the mind and that can be very dangerous. Now, are you agreeable to moving out of here?"

Her heart dropped to her stomach. He had no intention of sleeping with her, and she found his rejection stung. "Yes. What do I need to pack?"

He pushed himself out of the chair with powerful ease. "Pack light. It's hot where we're going."

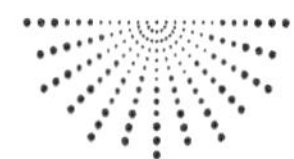

CHAPTER THREE

*C*rone snapped his fingers and filled the room with boxes of various sizes. "I suggest you start packing." His tone was a little terser than he'd meant. His cock had thickened with desire, and he was totally disgusted with himself. The girl had sought him out for help, and here his other head was trying to get in on the action.

Tessa looked around, her eyes wide. "Umm, I'm not planning on moving."

He picked up one of the smaller boxes and tossed it at her. "You don't have to use them all. You'll be living at my beach house but expect this might take some time. I'm not exactly sure yet what you want me to do other than protect you, but we can discuss that later." His gut told him killing the warlock wouldn't solve her problems. She was hiding something, and the best way for him to find out her secret would be to get her on his own turf. Perhaps he could seduce it out of her. Her body silently screamed its arousal, so teasing her into sharing what he wanted to know would be a simple task. Besides, he didn't have to follow through with sleeping with her. *Right. You're just looking for a way to drop her defenses.*

"Beach house?" she inquired.

"Yes, I own a private island."

She put the box on the coffee table and began setting some books inside. "How handy for you...having your own island."

"It has its perks." He watched as she placed the heavy leatherbound book on the top. "Interesting. So you think Zadicus will be unable to find me there?"

"Zadicus, I assume, is our warlock?"

She closed the box. "Got any tape? And yes, he would be the one coming after me."

"Can't you get your own tape? You're a witch, after all." He waited for her response, but she simply shrugged her shoulders and folded the box closed before she grabbed another.

"I assume I only need personal things?"

"Of course. What the?" He looked down to discover a black cat weaving in and out of his legs. "You didn't tell me you had a cat."

"Oh, that's Sebastian. He seems to like you." She tried to hide a giggle. "Don't you like cats?"

"That's not a cat. It's a creature pretending to be a cat." He snapped his fingers and summoned his own pet. "This is Ares."

She jumped back with a scream and scooped up the scraggly kitten, pulling it tight to her chest. "That's your pet?"

"Yes. You don't like Ares?"

"T-that's a damn tiger!"

"Of course, a real cat. Get used to her since she'll be roaming the island, helping to ensure your safety."

"But she'll eat Sebastian. Maybe even me!" She took another step back and bumped into the wall.

"Nonsense. She's fed and obeys my every command. Now, finish packing or leave with only the clothes on your back. Of course, you *are* a witch so certainly you can produce your own clothes." He patted Ares on the head.

Zadicus stared into a pool of azure, watching a Jinn move in on his territory. Not just any Jinn, but the one who had tortured then killed his grandfather. He spun and faced his demonling apprentice, Khrom. "A Jinn thinks he can best me?"

Khrom blinked, his ink-filled eyes stared at Zadicus. "Jinn are weak. You will go and take your female now?"

The warlock flipped the wool cape out of his way that warded off the chill and brushed past the demonling. Khrom, while young in demon years, was old compared to most. He held a vast knowledge of the world around him but apparently didn't realize exactly who this particular Jinn was.

"Khrom. Your assignment is to find any and all information you can on a Jinn named Crone." He passed his hands over the front of him, the demonling's clothes changing to jeans and a black button down shirt. "I'll be back."

He spread his fingers and waved his palms over the ground in front of him. Dirt and rock cracked and spread apart, leaving a gaping hole that he stepped into. Seconds later, he materialized inside Tessa's apartment, encased in invisible magic. Neither she nor her Jinn would be wise to the fact he stood in the corner and waited.

Zadicus was near. The marking on her shoulder burned in warning, but she couldn't know exactly where. Not until Ares fur bristled, and the tiger curled its lips revealing thick, sharp fangs.

Crone stiffened.

"He's near," she whispered.

"Bullshit. He's in the room with us," Crone announced and whispered something to the tiger by his side, causing the cat to promptly leap in front of Tessa. With the wall to her back, and a large cat at her front, she had no place to run.

"Show yourself, or do you fear the ass kicking you're going to receive?" Crone shouted.

Tessa clutched Sebastian tighter, and the kitten curled into her, not fighting. He likely sensed his best bet was right where he was.

Laughter. Sinister and dripping with danger, it filled the room, causing fear to twist her gut. Something told her this wouldn't end well. What did she truly know about Crone anyway? Only the legends, and she knew well enough how rumors started. Suddenly Zadicus shimmered into the corner.

"So this is how you treat me, Tessa? You dare bring another man into your home?" He stepped forward. "Correction. A human man I might abide but a Jinn? The lowest of the magical realm."

Hey, that Jinn happens to be my other half. Oh, where the hell did that come from? Being in close proximity to the man the ancestors had chosen for her did something to her head. *Yeah, it makes me stupid.*

Crone shoved out his chest and crossed his arms. Thick muscle rippled along his biceps, and for a moment, she melted at the sight of such strength. Zadicus, while handsome with long sliver-blond hair and dark grey eyes, was on the smaller side. Had she not known who he was and what he planned to do with her, he would have cut a seductive sight of his own.

The warlock tipped his head back in laughter while blue sparks flew from his fingertips. Never a good sign in the magic world, and she worried for all their safety. For a brief moment, she entertained the idea of giving herself over, but she had to trust Crone. She was far from ready to die.

A bright flash. A scream escaped her lips and everything went black. Heat encompassed her body and sweat beaded her forehead. A sudden jolt and she hit something hard. Blinking back tears, Tessa tried to regain her breath. A lead weight sat on her chest, crushing her. She was going to die. A blur of movement came into view as the light fought back the darkness.

She gasped.

This is how my life will end. A tiger, chewing my head off.

Ares straddled her. The big cat's golden eyes stared into hers, and its hot breath fanned over her face. Time stood still. Ares finally moved off her and sauntered across the room. Tessa sat up and frantically searched for Sebastian. The cat meowed and crawled into her lap, purring.

"Oh, thank god." She spied Ares again and watched, her jaw agape as the exquisite tiger transformed into an even more beautiful woman. "I... Oh my hell."

The tiger...er, woman smiled. Her gold-jeweled eyes, as brilliant as before, now framed by a messy mane of sable. She had high cheek-bones and full lips that would drive any man, and even some women, to their knees. Her bronzed skin, wrapped in a turquoise sari covered with silver beading, showed every curve.

"I'm a shifter," Ares announced in a sultry voice.

"I had no idea shifters really existed." Tessa stood, set down the kitty, and brushed herself off.

Ares moved with the grace of...well a tiger. "Our numbers have dwindled. I was rescued from my village where some humans had caged all the females and slaughtered the males. I'm unsure how many of the females escaped, but I know a few are hidden away. Crone has been my protector, and in return I help him where ever I can."

"I'm so sorry. How horrible that must have been for you." Tessa scanned the room. "Where is Crone? Did he not come with you?"

"He has yet to arrive. When the warlock presented himself I grabbed you and fled." Ares pushed aside a panel of creamy beige curtains to reveal a wall of glass doors. The beach shimmered like millions of tiny diamonds, and the contrast with the blue water hurt her eyes.

"This must be the island he spoke of?" Tessa moved closer to the glass.

"Yes. It's his favorite place, and I'm fortunate he allows me to live here. He visits often when he needs an escape from his home or the world in general." Ares began sliding the glass panels until the entire room opened to the outside. A warm, salty breeze wafted through the air but did nothing to warm Tessa.

"I hope I'm not causing you any inconvenience by staying here." Crone had assured her there was no female in his life she needed to worry about. However, she had to wonder how true that was. Ares was an exceptionally gorgeous woman, and if Crone hadn't already slept with her it could only mean he preferred men. Tessa already felt insecure about trying to seduce the Jinn, and now the woman beside her increased her doubt.

"I welcome the company of another female. Crone may know his way around a woman's body, but when it comes to other needs, he's clueless. He couldn't care less about what he refers to as idle chatter." She flashed a smile.

"Oh, so you and he are—"

"Friends with benefits?" Ares interrupted. "Yes, you could say that."

"Ahh, glad to see you two getting along," Crone called out, and both ladies spun to face him. Relief swept over Tessa that he was still in one piece, until the desire to claw his eyes out replaced it. Why was she jealous of Ares? *Maybe because she has more sex appeal in her little finger than I have in my entire body. And she can shift. I can't even get a spell right.*

Suddenly she noticed his burned shirt.

"Are you okay? What happened to Zadicus?" she asked, hoping the damn warlock was dead.

Crone strode across the wood floor. His boots made a heavy thud as he walked, all the while stripping off his scorched shirt and tossing it aside. Tessa folded her bottom lip through her teeth and bit down as she tried not to stare at the wall of muscle that stopped in front of her. Instead, she forced her focus upward and into a pair of blue eyes that danced with amusement.

"I'm fine."

He's not kidding.

"Your warlock is fine. Your apartment, however..." He lifted a shoulder and his pecs danced, beckoning her to touch. She smoothed her hands down her dress before she did something stupid. "I'm afraid it's trashed."

"What do you mean trashed?" she asked carefully.

He yanked the leather tie that bound his hair and shook it free. She nearly swallowed her tongue and again fought the urge to touch him, to slide her fingers through the shiny mass and comb it away from his face. Damn, she was in a shit load of trouble.

"I mean smashed furniture and holes in the walls. There may even be some singed carpet." He snorted. "I must admit, I haven't had this much fun in a long time."

Her jaw unhinged. "My apartment? You ruined all my stuff?" God she'd never be able to afford to replace everything. Not to mention what her landlord would do to her when she couldn't pay for the damages. "I don't look good in stripes and I hate orange!"

He tilted his head and furrowed his brows. "Excuse me?"

She pushed away from the glass and stomped across the room. "Prison stripes. Which is what I'll be wearing when my landlord gets done with me." She stopped and faced Crone and Ares. They both stared at her as if she were one card short of a deck. "What?"

Crone folded his arms, covering the view of his firm hard chest. *Damn.*

"You're a witch, or have you forgotten?" he asked.

"No." She rubbed her arms to ward off a chill that had nothing to do with the weather. "Don't be silly. You just took me by surprise is all." She was so screwed. If either Crone or Ares discovered her power, or lack thereof, who knew what they'd do.

CHAPTER FOUR

rone grew more suspicious of Tessa with each passing moment. Something wasn't right with that witch, and he intended to find out what she was hiding. "So, we need to talk." He eyed Ares and gave the silent command to leave them alone. The tiger shifter nodded and vanished, while he made his way to the fridge and yanked out a bottle of water. "Care for something?"

"No, thanks." She squared her shoulders and looked like she was preparing for battle. Awesome! He loved a good fight.

Crone chugged back half his water before he seductively wiped his hand across his lips. The look on her face said it all. She was ripe for seduction. "Sit," he commanded and pointed to the black leather sofa. She must have known not to press her luck because she scurried to comply, and he followed behind her. He bit his lip to keep from groaning out loud at the sway of her hips. The dark leather creaked as he took a seat next to her. She shifted her weight, pressing back into the corner. He focused on her lips.

She swiped her tongue across their plumpness in a nervous gesture, and he suddenly wondered what she tasted like.

"Tell me, *querida*. What do you expect out of this arrangement?" He lifted his gaze to focus on the brown depths of her eyes.

"I didn't know you were Spanish." She folded her hands onto her lap.

"My home is in the mists above Spain. Though technically my people are not Spanish, we're very fluent in the language and culture. Now, back to the arrangement."

"Arrangement?"

"Yes. You want me to protect you, but what else do you desire?" He moved in closer and brushed his finger down her cheek. Her lips parted, and he found himself leaning closer. The desire to kiss her overwhelmed him. "Do you want me to kill Zadicus for you? Will that solve your dilemma?"

"Umm. I-I hadn't thought about it, really. I suppose he would need to die, otherwise what's to stop him from coming after me again?"

Closer. Until his lips were only inches away from hers. "I know nothing would stop me if you were mine." That was no lie. For some reason this female brought out a nasty possessive streak, he'd not been aware he possessed. He watched her swallow hard and breathed in her musky arousal. His jeans tightened around his growing erection.

"I'm sure you always get what you want," she whispered.

He grinned. She had no idea how correct she was. He moved until his lips almost touched her ear. "I have my ways." His Spanish accent thicker than normal.

She shivered. "No doubt."

Leaning back, he jumped to his feet and noticed the disappointment on her face. The witch was putty in his hands, and he could and would mold her to his will. "Let me show you your room so you can settle in." Crone watched her stand and committed to memory her long legs, wide hips, and narrow waist. He also noted her hair; it had been straight earlier but now curled into a mass of silky black waves. "You should let your hair go natural. I like it better."

She lifted her hand to smooth it over her mane. "Oh, it must be the humidity in the air here." She blushed. "My hair is naturally curly, but I've always wanted it straight."

"May I ask you a personal question?" He stopped abruptly.

"Sure, I guess." He swore she paled.

"Are you able to do magic?"

Her eyes widened then shot sparks "I'm a witch, of course. Why would you ask?"

"Just curious." He shrugged and led her to the guest suite across from his own rooms. He held open the door and waved her in. "Your private rooms until we resolve your problem."

Tessa stepped into a room with thick, dark blue carpet and cream-colored walls. A large mural of a coral reef covered one side of the room and made her feel as if she were actually there. A small kitchenette occupied another side while a large blue couch and chairs faced the wall of glass door. A stone patio led right to the beach. She had a sudden urge to kick off her shoes and run through the sand.

"Wow. This is amazing."

"The bedroom is this way."

She followed Crone through a set of pocket doors that were partially open and into the bedroom. A king-size bed faced another wall of windows with a stunning view of the ocean and a private patio. An open doorway led through a short s-curve that revealed the master bath. Skylights flooded the room with sunshine, and Tessa couldn't help but notice the large walk-in shower was big enough for two.

Crone led her back out and to a set of double doors, which he flung open to showcase a large and rather stark walk-in closet.

"This obviously needs to be filled with clothes, shoes, whatever else you females like."

She nodded. "I think the closet is actually bigger than my apartment."

He grinned at her. "Fill it."

"Excuse me?"

"I said fill it with whatever you desire."

"Oh, of course. I'll do that later." She started to turn and leave the room.

"Now." There was no way to miss the command in his voice.

"What?"

His brows dipped into a furrow. "Do you not speak English? Prove to me that you have the ability to fill this closet with the essentials you need."

Shit! She was in some serious trouble. Apparently he suspected something, but she wasn't sure how or why. Did the blocking spell stop working? She had not tried any magic in his presence, and she wasn't about to start. Doing so could only lead to disaster. Instead, she lifted her chin. "Why do you insist? Shouldn't we be discussing what to do about Zadicus?" She turned her back and took a step, when she was suddenly halted by a large hand on her shoulder.

Crone spun her to face him.

"Either you fill this closet or I send you packing, and you can fend for yourself."

"Why is this so important to you?" *Double shit!* "It's only clothes for crying out loud." She was screwed either way because if she tried her magic and got her usual results, he would likely toss her out anyway. If she refused, she faced the same fate.

"It just is, so I suggest you start singing your chants and rubbing your charms, or whatever it is you witches do."

She wanted to be pissed. Oh hell, she was pissed, but he now had her backed into a literal corner with no place to run. She took in a deep breath to calm her nerves, but the opposite happened. His leather scent only boosted her sexual desire. *Pull your shit together, Tessa. It's only a damn closet full of clothes.* She closed her eyes, searched for the words, and ran them through her mind. Magic circled her and caused her skin to prickle. *Something's happening.* She cracked open one eye, afraid to see what she'd done but was pleasantly surprised.

"There. Happy now?" She placed her hands on her hips in satisfaction.

Crone looked into the closet and back at her. A brow lifted. "You call that pittance a closet full?"

"I don't need much. Besides, I hate to waste," she retorted, so done with this whole mess.

He cocked his head. "One pair of jeans and ten yellow tank tops is your idea of clothing?"

She lifted her chin. "Flip flops. Did you not notice the flip flops?"

He crossed his arms, biceps bulging, and leaned back on his heels. "Unless fashion has taken a drastic change, one still needs a matching pair which is not what you have." His mouth curled in amusement.

She did a double take and looked down at the lone pair of sandals. One was bright pink with a silk flower on top and the other pale blue and made of terry. It was a damn bedroom slipper. "Shit." She muttered and Crone's amusement turned to full-blown laughter.

"I don't need shoes anyway. After all, this is a beach," she laced her voice with all the sarcasm she could muster.

His laughter died as quickly as it started, and he leveled his gaze. "Why don't you tell me the truth. You don't have a handle on your magic."

"Don't be absurd." Before she could react, he had her caged to the wall and unable to move. If he stood any closer, they would touch in the most intimate way. She slammed her palms on his chest and shoved.

Nothing.

"You want me to move? You'll have to make me. I may be physically stronger than you, but you're a witch. You must have something in that bag of tricks of yours."

Tessa's face heated, and she commanded a jolt of energy to her fingertips. When nothing happened, she panicked. Her heart raced faster when she was greeted by a mooing sound, and Crone's eyes widened. He released her and spun to face the disturbance.

She pushed up on her tiptoes and peered over his shoulder. "Oh, hell."

He craned his neck to look back at her. "Really? That's it? Oh, hell?"

"Sorry?" She gave a weak smile.

"There's a fucking cow in the middle of the bedroom!" He walked toward the creature; words she didn't understand poured from his mouth, but she was pretty sure she was better off clueless. Suddenly the cow raised its tail and let loose a steaming pile. Tessa covered her mouth and nose, but it failed to help.

"I'm more sorry than you know," she mumbled through her hand.

Crone simply flicked his wrist and both the cow and its offending gift were gone. He pointed toward the door. "Go plant your ass in a chair, and this time if you insist on lying to me like a damn child then I will treat you like one." A devilish grin plastered his face. "I will put you across my knee and paddle your ass like my father used to do to me when I created havoc."

Tessa's eyes were as wide as saucers, and she practically ran through the door and sat in the chair closest to the patio. Did she think to plan an escape? Crone chuckled to himself. It was difficult to be too angry with her, but he wouldn't go easy on her. This could be a matter of life and death, mainly hers. Damn, he still had this sensation she was hiding something from him.

He planted himself in front of her so she had to look up. He'd conjured a shirt since he was done trying to seduce her, intent on scaring her instead. "How much control do you have over your magic?" She licked her lips, and he tried not to moan. The woman really had no clue the effect she had on the male species. Just the idea another man might carry the same thoughts about her pissed him off.

With a heavy sigh, she explained, "It pretty much has a mind of its own a good share of the time."

"I see. That explains a few things. Does it ever work?" Hurt filled her eyes. He was suddenly riddled with guilt, but he didn't apologize.

"Yes."

Why did he not believe her? "Tessa, you need to be completely honest. I don't want to get into a situation where this could cause us trouble."

"I'm just rusty is all. Besides, am I not safe here?"

He was edgy, so he began to pace. "Of course, the island is protected by magic. That doesn't mean, however, that Zadicus can't still find you and break through my barriers. He's very powerful and something tells me he'll stop at nothing to get what he wants." He paused. "Matter of fact, when I'm not here, I'll have my brother Lazaro come and hang out."

"What about Ares? I thought she was going to help protect me?" She shifted in her seat.

"She will, but she can only do so much. Ares is good at battle, but magic is something she can't fight against." He went and knelt in front of her. "Look, it's obvious Zadicus has to die, but will that break your curse?"

Tessa shifted her gaze away from him and stared out the bank of windows. "It will free me from Zadicus' bond, but another male in his family could come for me. If not me, then my daughter will suffer the same fate. The curse needs to be broken."

"Look at me Tessa." He waited for her to turn her head and focus on him. "Do you know how to break this curse?"

"Yes."

Silence filled the room. Apparently, she wasn't willing to share. "Care to tell me?"

"Not really."

"Woman, you are backing me into a corner." He knew he should simply walk away. Kill the damn warlock, collect his gold, and be done. Why should he care if her family curse was removed? She'd not hired him for more than protection, so technically he could keep her under his roof and never kill Zadicus since that wasn't mentioned when he was hired. Crone never had any problems before being a kept Jinn. Everyone knew what his passions were. Gold, women, and war, not necessarily in that order, but one usually led to the other. His guilt however, had other things to say on the matter. Tara––he could see her look of disapproval for not protecting her family.

Damn, will that female ever stop haunting me?

"I really think you should re-consider." He got up to leave.

CHAPTER FIVE

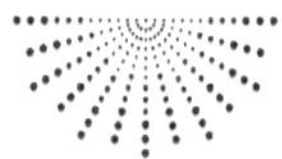

$\mathcal{T}$essa's gut clenched as Crone got up and started to walk away. She needed him, but how could she expect him to help her if she hid the truth?

"Wait!"

He stopped, but didn't turn around, so she hopped out of her chair and slipped up behind him. Fear kept her from stepping in front to face him head on. "Tara gave you her magic before she died."

He did a slow turn. "What? I thought Morden took that from her?"

She squared her shoulders. Damn it, she would not be afraid of him. "When our virginity is taken, our power can be jerked from us. It's what the Demois men do. It was what Morden did as well. My Nana was a very powerful witch and somehow she still had power when she died. She passed it to you."

Crone shook his head as if he had cobwebs that needed removing. "Wait... I would have known if Tara had given me her power. I felt no surge of magic."

"Of course you wouldn't. It's masked to protect both parties involved."

He narrowed his gaze. "How can you be sure of this?"

"Mother told me."

"So what does it mean, and why would she do that?"

Tessa pulled in a breath. "She did it in hopes someone in the family line would be able to break the curse. She knew that special witch would need her extra power."

He gave her a sideways glance. "Let me guess. You're that witch."

Tessa nodded. "I was born on the Harvest moon, therefore I can take back her power and break the spell that started this curse." He lifted his chin and crossed his arms over that expansive chest she wanted so badly to run her fingertips across.

"You can't produce enough clothes to fill a closet, yet you're supposed to break a curse?"

That stung but she refused to let on. "Yes."

"Why do I feel there's more?"

She chewed her bottom lip and looked around the room as if someone would step out and help her. Save her from embarrassment.

"Well?"

"You...uhh. You have to take my virginity."

He blinked but remained silent, until his gaze turned cold and drilled into her like two icicles. "Sorry. Not happening."

Hell. How was she supposed to respond to that? Telling him she was his mate was out of the question, so she would have to suck it up and ask. "Why not?"

"For one I don't know you," came his condescending reply.

She snorted. "Really? I find it hard to believe you have morals when it comes to sleeping with women." She watched hurt flash to anger in his eyes.

"That's right. After all, I'm a Jinn warrior and used to taking what I want. I like it fast and rough." He curled his lip. "Something I doubt you could handle. Virgins are too...delicate." He turned and stormed away, but she wasn't letting him or this go.

"Don't you dare insult me then walk away," she cried out.

"Or what?" He shouted over his shoulder, never breaking stride. "Will you cast some kind of spell on me or perhaps turn the house into a barnyard?"

"Low blow."

"Maybe, but I speak the truth. Don't I?" He walked back into the living room.

"You're a jackass." She felt her face heat and realized her nails dug into her palms. He spun to face her, all riled-up male, and damn if he wasn't sexy as hell.

"That the best you got?" He glared. Why the hell was he so pissed at her?

"Oh, I've got a lot more, but what are we arguing about and what do we hope to gain?" Tessa was not a fighter. She hated confrontation.

"We're arguing because you can't take rejection. I'll kill the warlock, but you'd better figure out another way to get your power back from me, because fucking you is not an option." He headed for the glass doors, pulling his shirt off and tossing it as he went. She had to stifle a moan at the ripple of back muscle.

"Stop walking away from me." She cursed under her breath and started after him.

✿

Crone heard a screech behind him and jerked around to find Tessa on the floor clutching her foot, writhing in pain. "What the hell?" He was at her side in an instant.

"It's nothing," she replied through clenched teeth.

"Your foot is already swelling. Don't tell me it's nothing." He reached to touch her, but she jerked away. Okay, he got it. He'd been an ass. He scanned the room then it dawned on him. "You tripped over the coffee table?"

She squeezed her eyes shut. "I'm a klutz, all right?"

He sighed. "By the looks of it I'd say your toe is broken."

"No shit!"

With another sigh, he scooped her up and headed toward the bedroom. Thoughts of baseball and every other thing he could think of swept through his mind as he tried to keep his erection deflated. Her curves fit against him as if they were made to, and he couldn't help notice how silky her skin was. His anger began to surface; he didn't understand why he had trouble keeping his libido under control in her presence.

"What are you doing?"

"I'd think it's obvious. Did you hit your head too?" He couldn't help the sarcasm.

"Funny." She feigned laughter. "Ow. I think you're right, my toe's broke." Her skin paled, and he grew concerned.

"I'm summoning a healer." When she raised a brow, he cut her off. "Don't worry. My younger brother has a special talent and should have you on your feet in—"

"No time," Lazaro replied from behind them.

"Ah, what took you so long?" Crone asked.

His sibling rolled his eyes and headed to the bed where Crone had propped Tessa against several pillows. "Hi, I'm Lazaro the more charming of the brothers."

Crone snorted, but when he witnessed the huge smile Tessa flashed his sibling, a sudden urge to throttle the youngest Jinn in his family came over him. The fact he wanted to do so pissed him off even more. Jealousy wasn't even in his vocabulary. Least not until today, not until Tessa. *Damn witch.* "Can you just get on with healing her? And while you're at it, maybe you can fix her clumsiness."

Tessa folded her arms. "Maybe you can make your brother less of an ass."

Lazaro chuckled. "I see you two are getting along fine. Unfortunately, there's no cure for Crone's arrogance."

It was Tessa who snorted this time. "I'm not surprised."

"I didn't summon you here for insults. Fix the damn witch," Crone growled, his anger and impatience ever increasing.

"This will sting a bit." Lazaro placed his hand on the swollen and now purple foot. Crone felt magic stir in the air as his brother knitted her broken bone back together. Tessa bit her lip and winced, but she never cried out. Crone admired her backbone, but it didn't stop him from wanting to pull her into his lap and comfort her.

His annoyance flared again.

After several minutes, she was able to wiggle her toes, and Lazaro stepped back to admire his handiwork. "While it's healed you should stay off it for at least a day. The swelling will take that long to go completely down. My brother would be honored to wait on you hand and well...foot." He chuckled.

"Thank you. It feels better already. I do think I could use a nap though." She tried to stifle a yawn.

"Rest. We'll leave you alone." Lazaro pushed Crone toward the door. When they were both outside, Crone nearly came unglued.

"What the fuck? I am not--read my lips--not becoming her servant." Crone shook, but he wasn't sure if it was from anger or the thought of her lying in bed naked. *And where the hell did that come from?*

"You'll do whatever you want, but try being nice to the poor girl."

"Why do you care all of a sudden about my house guests?"

Lazaro headed outside and stepped into the sun, tipped his face up, and closed his eyes. "She's a beauty, Crone. So what have you learned? I gather by the exchange of dialogue in there, you're attracted to her." He turned his head and partially opened one eye to glare at Crone.

"Fucker."

"I've always loved your pet names," Lazaro laughed.

"She is Tara's granddaughter."

"Ah." Lazaro stared at him. "Your guilt is showing again."

"You should consider *not* taking up becoming a therapist because you suck at it." Crone skirted by his brother, sand spreading under his boots, as he stormed around the outside of the house to reach the glass doors Once through them, he headed straight for the fridge and jerked it open. He shoved aside the bottles of water and reached for a brew. Twisting off the cap, he flicked it at his brother as he entered the room and tipped back the icy beverage. Bitter cold coated his throat, but it did nothing to break the sweat that had formed on his brow. *What the hell is wrong with me?*

"The female has you rattled."

"Don't be absurd," Crone shot back. "Don't you have someplace else to be?"

His sibling grinned. "Yes, dear brother, I do. Try not to blow the place up with your temper. I'll check in tomorrow to see how the patient is." He vanished. Crone sighed and took another swig of his beer. He really did need a shrink.

Crone had left Tessa in the capable hands of Ares, while he went back to the house of Tujan, his native home in the mists above Spain. He sat at his desk, trying to put together a plan on how to locate and kill Tessa's warlock. His thoughts were interrupted when Lazaro and Armand entered the room.

Crone looked up from his paperwork.

"Greetings, brother," the two Jinn spoke in unison.

He eyed his siblings with suspicion. "Greetings. Why do I get the feeling this isn't a social call?"

Armand slipped into the chair across from him. "Because it's not. We are here to help you track and kill the warlock."

"Obviously you've been chatting with your lovely wife." Crone motioned Lazaro to the other chair.

"I'll stay back here. You may wish to kill me in about ten seconds," Lazaro responded.

"What did you do?" he inquired.

"He told me about your time with Morden and about Tara," Armand answered.

Crone shot out of his chair, but before he could reach his youngest––soon to be dead sibling––Armand grabbed him and pinned his feet to the floor with his magic. "Release me so I can rip him to shreds. How dare you divulge my secrets!" While Crone wouldn't really kill his little brother, he could make him hurt.

"Stand down, and I'm not asking," Armand commanded.

Crone met his eldest brother's gaze, and while he wanted to challenge Armand, he had enough respect for the older Jinn's authority. "Only because you command it." He relaxed and Armand released his magic. Crone took his seat, but leveled a death glare on the youngest Jinn in the room.

"Don't blame him. Father caught wind that you were hired by a witch to protect her from some warlock and grew worried. He and Lazaro came to me and they both spilled what happened." Armand gestured for Lazaro to sit. "He will not harm you."

"Father." Crone sighed.

Armand leaned forward, resting his elbows on the desk. "Damn it, Crone. Why'd you hide this from me? All those times you came to visit when I was bound to earth. Gave me shelter when the humans of the village would grow suspicious when I never aged. What did all of that cost you?"

Crone didn't look away. "It matters not what the price was. I would have paid anything to see to your comforts."

Armand didn't flinch. "The truth, brother. How did you end up an assassin to a warlock?"

He thought of concocting a tale, but knew Armand would see through it. He always did and since he was now aware of what Crone had done, it was best to get everything out in the open. "In order to get Cyndel to agree to let me see you, I had to become Morden's slave."

"Shit," Lazaro whispered. Both his brother and father always believed he'd been captured, not gone willingly.

"It was your visits that kept me going. When you saved Kayla..."Armand choked a little

Crone held up his hand. He was never good at the mushy shit. "Stop. I did nothing more than I would have done for father or Lazaro. Family is all that matters."

Both brothers nodded in agreement. "That's why we're here. To help you with this little problem," This time Armand held up his hand. "And we expect nothing in return––only that you let go of your guilt."

Crone would like nothing more than to have some peace, but it wasn't happening. "It's my pain to carry."

"Crone, you did what you could to save the witch," Lazaro replied.

Crone stood so fast his chair rolled back and hit the wall. He slammed his fists on the desk. "I did no such thing. Tara still died at the hand of Morden because of my arrogance. You were not the one to hold her in your arms and watch her take her last breath. Your clothes were not stained with her blood. I know I spent years killing for Morden and that I will carry as well, but there was something about Tara. That witch never showed an ounce of fear and I failed her."

He relaxed slightly. "I appreciate the offer, but I will do this alone. I owe the girl that much." He owed Tessa much more than he could repay, but he'd start with giving her some peace by killing her pursuer. She'd offered to pay for his service, but this one was on him. As for the small problem with her gaining Tara's magic back... There had to be another way. Hell would freeze over before he'd be able to look her in the eyes and not feel the sting of guilt. He had this nagging feeling that if he ever did have Tessa, he'd never let her go.

CHAPTER SIX

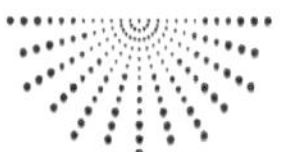

essa opened her eyes and wiped the sleep from them. Sunlight and a warm ocean breeze blew through the open glass doors. She sat up and noticed a tray at the foot of the bed. A coffee carafe, mug, and a plate filled with strawberries, various melon slices, pineapple, and blueberries called to her. She let her feet hit the floor then padded over and poured herself a cup of coffee. After adding cream and sugar, she took a sip.

"Ohh, this is good." Turning to face the open doors, she spotted a form down by the water's edge. Moving out the door to stand on the stone patio, she focused to get a better look.

"Oh my lord." The most firm, round, muscular naked male ass she'd ever laid eyes on stood on the beach, and it was attached to a body that rivaled any Greek God of mythology. By the long black hair flowing down his back, she knew it was Crone. Looking away was not an option—not that she wanted to—but it would be the polite thing to do. "Screw manners." Besides, being his destined mate had to come with some perks. Didn't it? Even if she didn't intend to follow through with it.

She set her mug on a nearby table as she moved across the patio and into the sand. *I must get a closer look.* Suddenly he turned and looked at her over his shoulder as he stepped into the waves and removed her magnificent view.

"Damn it." She went back and picked up her mug, taking a sip of coffee when she got the feeling someone watched her. With a slow turn, she faced a wet Crone. Clad only in a towel, rivulets of water followed every peak and valley of muscle and sinew. She could hardly swallow, her tongue thick, wanting to lick him dry like a damn cat. For a moment, she wondered what it might be like to wake up next to him every morning.

"I wanted to apologize for yesterday."

She blinked and reminded herself to keep her gaze focused on his. "Thank you. Apology accepted."

"I will do what I can to protect you. I'll hunt Zadicus, end his miserable life, and accept no payment in return."

Holy hell. Had she been wrong about him? She tried to hide her relief at not having to pay him gold she didn't have. "Why would you do that?"

"I failed your grandmother, therefore I owe you both. I only ask for one thing."

"What's that?"

"I can't take your virginity. You must understand that it's not personal. You're a beautiful woman and deserve to give that to the man you love. One who will worship the very ground you walk on. Please tell me there's another way to end your curse." For one moment, he looked like a lost little boy instead of the strong Jinn that many had grown to fear over the ages. The urge to comfort him flooded her, but she dared not touch him. It was obvious that what happened between her Nana and him still caused him a great deal of pain. She couldn't respect a man more than she did at this moment. She almost spilled who she really was but thought better of it. He'd likely freak out at the news anyway.

"There is another way. It's complicated and not guaranteed to work." She sighed. "With my magic having a mind of its own, I'm not sure I have the strength to do it alone."

His eyes fired up. "What is it? If I can lend my power in any way, count me in." He snapped his fingers and to her dismay, he was dry and dressed in a pair of shorts. At least he still allowed her a view of his bare chest.

Tessa moved to one of the wicker chairs and took a seat. "There's a spell that can be performed on the next hunter's moon. We need Zadicus' blood, a lock of hair, and the piece of skin that carries the moon symbol. Oh, and he needs to be alive."

Crone nodded as if this was all in a day's work for him. "What else?"

"I'd need to draw power from you. It would require the mixing of our blood and allow us to combine power for a brief period." This was exactly why she'd not mentioned it earlier. She might have been able to get away with having sex with him, using a blocking spell so he'd not discover she was his mate. However, mixing blood...there was no way around that one and he'd know in an instant.

"The hunter's moon will be here in a couple of days, so how fresh do you need your items to be?"

"Uh, anytime would be fine. Do you know where Zadicus is?" Finding the warlock might prove to be impossible right now. Tessa knew the warlock was also aware of how to break the bond and would go into hiding.

Crone rubbed his goatee and stared off for several minutes before responding. "My minions haven't had any luck yet."

Tessa felt her brows shoot upward. "Minions?"

He shrugged as if it meant nothing. "I have creatures who spy for me. No one has seen the bastard, but he will be located. I have my best tracker on it."

"And who would that be?"

"Ares of course. Nothing better than a tiger to find your enemy." His lip curled upward, and for some reason Tessa felt a pang of jealousy over the beautiful shifter who seemed to hold a great deal of Crone's admiration. The mention of Ares name must be magical on its own. The large cat leaped through the air, coming from some invisible portal, and landed at Crone's feet where she rubbed her massive head against his leg. He reached down to scratch between her ears, and Tessa gritted her teeth.

"Ah beautiful, speak of the feline. Have you had any luck yet?" The cat curled at his feet and focused its big eyes on Tessa. She could swear she saw hatred lurking in their amber depths. But why? It wasn't like Tessa had staked any claims on Crone. Though she would be within her right to do so.

The cat continued to stare then pushed out its large pink tongue and licked the edge of its lips as if to intimidate. Ares was successful; Tessa touched her throat and looked away.

"I don't think she likes me," she whispered as if an animal with far superior hearing than her own wouldn't hear her. *Dumb ass.*

"Who? Ares? Don't be silly. She has no reason to dislike you." His lids dropped to slits. "Unless you did something to harm her?"

Mental note. The Jinn definitely has a protective streak for the tiger. "Of course not. She just looks as if she'd like to devour me."

He laughed. "She wants to eat every one. Let's go inside and form a plan to find this warlock, so I can skin him alive."

Crone headed into the house with Ares still in her tiger form hot on his heels.

I'm not sure I trust her.

Why? Has she done something to you?

No, it's only a feeling I have.

He patted the cat on the head. *Unless she does something to harm you or I, then you must give her a chance.* Ares had never trusted strangers easily, and she got a little twitchy when he got too close to other females. At least her cat did. Crone sometimes thought Ares wanted more, but he valued her friendship and didn't want to do anything to jeopardize that. Besides, she was more like a sister to him than someone to have a sexual relationship with.

Perhaps you should go fetch my brothers for me. Tell them to meet me on the far side of the beach at nightfall.

Fine. Ares jumped into the air and vanished.

"Where's she going?" Tessa had snuck in now that Ares had left.

"I sent her with a message to my brothers. I'll have them help me track Zadicus, starting tonight." He picked up the coffee carafe that had been left in her room and poured himself a cup. "You haven't touched your food."

She picked up a strawberry. "I got sidetracked."

He kept his smile at bay, knowing *he'd* been the distraction. It pleased him. "Eat and keep your strength up. I may need your help in finding Zadicus." He didn't want to involve her since it was dangerous, but if left with no alternatives, he'd do what needed to be done to capture the warlock.

"Any way I can help?" She shoved the tip of the berry between her lips, and he could swear she batted her lashes. Damn it to hell and back. Why did he feel like a smitten teen when around this witch?

"Any idea where he might hide?"

She bit, chewed, and licked her lips before speaking. "I wish I did, but I have a thought on how to bring him into the open."

"And you were planning to tell me when?"

She lifted a shoulder. "You might be opposed, and I didn't want to tick anyone off."

This woman was a curious creature and the more he was around her, the more interested he became. "I'm not sure who you'd be pissing off, but let me be the judge on whether I oppose."

"I basically have a magical chastity belt. If I become too sexually aroused by another male then Zadicus will show up to defend his virgin."

Crone spit out the gulp of coffee he'd just taken. "What? Let's back up a moment. I seem to recall an earlier conversation where I was to take your virginity. How the hell did you plan for that to happen?"

"Umm. I'd planned to use a blocking spell."

Good lord! Crone was thankful he'd had enough sense to stay away from her. "And you expected that to work when as far as I've seen, your magic sucks?" Harsh but true.

Tessa shuffled her feet. "I know, I'm a klutz. My magic only works part-time, and I don't always think things through, but I was smart enough to get the spell from a more reliable witch."

She lifted her gaze, and he swore there were unshed tears. "I'm a poor excuse for a witch, and the sad thing is I don't know why. I mean I can understand why my magic wouldn't be as strong as it should, but there's no reason it shouldn't work at all."

Now he felt like a real ass. "I don't know a lot about witches, but I understand you require a familiar to help you with your magic." He glanced around. "Speaking of, where is the kitten?"

"Sebastian? Likely curled up under the covers napping. He's not my familiar and yes, having one would strengthen my magic. However, the lack of one isn't why my spells seem to have a mind of their own."

He pondered that statement for a moment, and it did make sense. "We'll have to come back to that later. In the meantime, getting you aroused will bring on the warlock?"

She turned a pretty shade of pink. "Yes."

"I can do that. We'll rendezvous on the beach where my brothers can hide and set a trap." With a plan in place, and the day half gone, he left her to shower and get ready while he plotted how to contain a pissed warlock. He had to admit, he was looking forward to seeing how Tessa responded to his ministrations. He had a feeling she'd be even more beautiful when aroused.

Tessa wore a thin dress that showed off her long, shapely legs. She'd left her hair loose, and the raven curls bounced in the ocean breeze. The sun had begun its decent and danced over the tops of the waves, throwing bursts of orange and red across the landscape.

Shit. Crone was beginning to think her plan was crazy or he was. Either way, he was screwed. Armand, Lazaro, and Ares hid in the background behind the sand dunes and waited to spring the trap once Zadicus showed.

"Are you certain this will work?" he asked. She stepped closer until he could smell gardenias. How had he not realized before that she smelled like an exotic flower? She awakened his senses and placed them on full alert.

"Only if we make it real enough. Simply kissing me won't bring Zadicus here. We need to put as much heat into this as possible. He needs to feel my virginity is threatened," she answered and placed her palm on his bare chest.

Double shit. "I hold a degree in heat."

"I'll be the judge of that." Her smile nearly melted him.

"Don't fear." He pulled her to him and nipped at her ear. "I'll have you begging me to fuck you within minutes."

"You're so vulgar and sure of yourself," she stated, yet her arousal already began to mingle with her floral scent.

Crone took her words as a challenge He loved a challenge, never backed down from one. He cupped her ass, lifted her so their lips met, and brushed a delicate kiss across her mouth. She tasted like the morning dew. Fresh and clean. He nipped at her bottom lip and ran his tongue along the seam of her mouth until her lips parted with a moan. Before she would have a chance to think, he slipped in his tongue. It swept, swirled, and dueled with hers. Heat built between them, and he pressed her to his growing erection. She wrapped her legs around his waist and ground into him.

Dirty wench. She was trying to seduce him back.

He pulled free, sucking her bottom lip as he broke off the kiss. He licked and nipped her jaw, making his way along the sensitive flesh down her neck until he hit the secret spot at the top of her shoulder. She threw her head back with a cry and ground into him harder.

Perfect.

Her nipples jutted through the thin material, and she hadn't worn a bra. He lowered his head and sucked a nipple through her flimsy dress. Her nails dug into his flesh and spurred him on further.

Passion ignited between them. For a moment, he forgot where they were, and that this was only a ploy to unleash the fury of a warlock.

"Unhand her!"

Crone slammed back to the present and thank the gods. He wasn't sure he would have stopped. He wanted to press her body into the sand, take her right there on the beach and witnesses be damned. Instead, he shoved her behind him and glared at the warlock. Killing Zadicus would be too good for the warlock who meant to hurt his witch. It all made sense now: his mood swings, his possessiveness over her, and the unquenchable desire. He wasn't sure if she was aware of it, or if this was the secret she'd been trying to hide, but kissing her had unlocked everything. Tessa belonged to him.

CHAPTER SEVEN

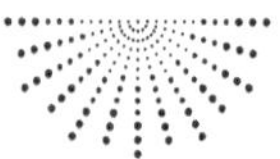

*T*essa had risen to a rapid boil when Crone kissed her. She'd suspected he might be good, but *damn.* When he'd sucked her nipple through the fabric of her dress, her entire body melted while his hardened further against her. She'd forgotten for a moment where they were and that his brothers were watching...waiting. The sound of that sinister voice yelling had jerked her back to reality so hard her head spun.

Zadicus was here and his anger could be felt in the tattoo on her shoulder. *Shit!* She'd been so involved in Crone's seduction, she hadn't even noticed the warning signs of the approaching warlock. All she could do now was pray their plan worked.

Shouts rang in the air as Crone shoved her behind him. She fell to the ground, the sand softening the blow. The surf washed over her legs, and she struggled to get back to her feet. Power zinged across her skin, but it didn't hold the evil oily feel of Zadicus. Instead, it was warm and silky, and she knew it belonged to Crone. He was trying to protect her. Tessa lifted her head to see what was happening, but smoke and flashes of light filled the darkening sky.

"Crone?" she coughed.

There was no reply, but she spotted Lazaro, the youngest brother...

Shifting? Did he just turn into smoke? She blinked, thinking it must have been her imagination, and he'd simply vanished. A thunderous boom pierced her eardrums. Sand shot several feet into the air only inches away from her, a gaping hole left in its wake. Tessa shuddered. "Holy hell." She began to crawl, keeping her head low, but had no idea where she was headed. *Outta here before I get my ass zapped!*

A blast of white light shot in her path. She did a quick about face and ran into something large and furry. Slowly lifting her head, she peered up at a huge tiger. "Ares." The cat shifted, and the woman kneeled, extending her hand.

"Hurry, I must get you out of here before you're harmed."

Tessa sighed. "Thank the ancestors." She placed her hand in the woman's palm, and the sounds began to drift away. The smoke cleared, and she took in a lungful of clean air. "Where are we going?"

"Somewhere safe"

A dimly lit room came into focus, and she could swear she heard waves crashing in the distance. Once her vision cleared, she found herself inside a large room. The scent of the sea hung thick in the air and came through the open windows that surrounded the room. The floor was covered with large flagstones and thick carpets that looked like they needed a good shaking out. Furniture, draped in white sheets, were scattered about. It was obvious the place hadn't seen any life in some time.

"Where are we?"

Ares walked to a window and looked out; Tessa followed her. She was startled to find they were high above the ocean, perched on a cliff in what she could only guess was some sort of castle. "Oh that's a long way down."

Ares faced her. "This place has been abandoned for centuries, but I've tried to keep it up as best I could. It once belonged to my ancestors." Sadness filled her eyes. "They are all gone now. Crone is all I have left."

"I'm sorry, Ares." Fear prickled her skin. Something wasn't right. "We shouldn't have left the others. They may need our help." When she'd left, she'd been unable to determine who was winning and now her concern for Crone grew. The Jinn was an arrogant ass, yet she was able to look deeper and see his pain. Somehow, he needed to realize he had not failed Tara, and Tessa had to make him see that. There was also the fact he was growing on her.

Ares backed away. "I'm sorry, but you have to stay here. You can't have Crone, he doesn't belong to you."

Tessa's heart jumped into her throat. "What are you saying?" Her gaze darted around the room looking for... What? She had no idea. Escape? Hell, she didn't even know where she was. "Ares?" Panic filled her voice.

"There's plenty of provisions here for you. You'll be safe, but know that there is a spell keeping the castle hidden. No one will find you." Ares shifted and bounded through the archway. Tessa took off after her.

"Ares!" She ran through several rooms. Many with the same white cloth covering the furniture, but they all blurred together. When she finally came to a set of large, wooden double doors, she grasped the handle on one and prayed. The door opened to the outside and she stepped into the sun, but rather than feel its warmth she shivered. Magic like she'd never experienced before pulsed all around her. She was trapped, and a witch as weak as her would never break through the barrier.

Crone had two out of three. He'd drawn blood and even managed to rip a hunk of hair from Zadicus's head. However, the skin that held the tattoo wasn't part of his prized collection. The bastard had managed to escape.

"I've never encountered a warlock who could best three Jinn," Armand spoke, wiping the sweat from his brow.

They'd battled long and hard. Crone's beach looked like it had been pelted by asteroids. Craters littered the once pristine sand. He'd clean it up later. Right now he needed to make sure Tessa was safe. He'd lost track of her, but assumed Ares had taken her to safety.

"Zadicus couldn't have been acting alone. He was far too power-ful," Crone replied. "Have you seen Tessa?"

"I saw her and Ares together earlier," Lazaro piped up.

Crone brushed sand off his jeans. "Good." Relieved for the moment, he was anxious to clean things up, find Tessa, and talk to her. Did she know what she was? That question nagged at him. "Help me clean this place up." He'd have to pull together a plan later on how to get the tattoo off the warlock. He would do it though, even if he had to skin the bastard alive. The trouble was that now he had to locate him. Crone secretly wondered if seducing Tessa again would bring the same results.

Give up the thought of having her. He'd failed to protect her grand-mother. How could she not hate him for his failure now? What did he have to offer her? The only thing that might bring either of them a sense of peace was killing the entire Demois clan. Now that would bring him immense pleasure.

He shook himself back to the present and shoved his skeletons into their closet. He would set his sights on presenting Tessa with Zadicus's head. Every fiber of his being screamed to protect her at all costs.

After an hour of intense magic, he and his brothers had put the beach back to its original state and not a spec of sand was out of place. Armand and Lazaro had gone home. Crone shifted to smoke and let the ocean breeze carry him back toward the house. Halfway there, he came across Ares and swirled around her then shifted back.

"Ares. Where's Tessa?" The girl blinked as if she hadn't understood him.

"I thought she was with you."

His body went rigid. "No. You mean to tell me you've not seen her?"

Ares nodded. "I was with her briefly, but I took her back to the house while I chased a demon."

"You left her alone?" Crone shifted and was off like a shot, pushing himself to fly faster until he finally reached the house and shifted as he entered through the open glass door. "Tessa?" He ran to the room he'd given her and shoved open the door. Only Sebastian greeted him with a meow and a rub on his leg.

"Fuck!" He spun and nearly ran into Ares. "Any luck?"

"I'm afraid the house is empty."

His heart skipped several beats. He stalked around Ares, back to the main living area where he lifted a glass end table off the floor and flung it across the room. Enjoying the sound of it shattering to bits, he worked his jaw until it ached. "He fucking has her," he spat. "God knows what the fucker is doing to her." He turned to Ares. "Why did you not protect her as instructed?" If Zadicus was anything like his sick father, Crone could imagine what was happening to his mate. Bile rose in his throat. A soft hand touched his arm, and he looked into Ares golden eyes.

"I'm so sorry. I thought she'd be safe here."

Ares had never failed him before, and Crone grew suspicious. He had to shove it aside for now because Tessa was his top priority.

"I have to find her, Ares. If I have to rip apart every realm in existence, I have to find her."

❀

Tessa walked the entire perimeter of the castle, searching for any break in the magic where she might be able to squeeze out. Whoever had erected the barrier was powerful and not from a species she recognized. Finally, she gave up and went back inside to explore, hoping there would be some kind of clue to help her.

She was surprised to find a modern kitchen with stainless steel appliances big enough to entertain a large crowd. Granite counters lined the outside perimeter, while a butcher-block island as big as her own kitchen took center stage. It was totally out of place in the ancient castle.

In the middle was a crystal bowl filled with apples, oranges, pears, and bananas. Hunger rumbled in her stomach and she grabbed an apple then headed to the fridge.

"I guess Ares wasn't kidding when she said this place was stocked."

She fetched a bottle of water and made a mental note to come back later for something more substantial. Providing of course she was still stuck here. Tessa held onto the hope either Ares would come to her senses and come back for her, or Crone would find her. In the meantime, she'd make the best of a horrendous situation. A gut wrenching thought came to her. What if Crone was also behind this? What if he had realized Tessa was his mate, and the only way he saw to be with Ares was to lock Tessa away? She shook her mind free of the heart-stopping thoughts. She had to stay positive.

Picking her way back through the rooms she'd entered when chasing after Ares, she stopped dead in her tracks. She blinked. "I'm positive the furniture was covered when I..." Realization dawned. "Ares?" she yelled. Tessa ran to the library and discovered everything uncovered there, too.

"Hello?" Chills pimpled her spine.

"Good evening, Tessa."

Tessa whirled to face the soft voice that had spoken her name. She stared at a beautiful woman, slightly taller than her height of five feet seven. Her shoulder-length hair, midnight black tipped with red, framed a porcelain complexion with brilliant green eyes. Her dress matched her eyes and flowed to the floor.

"Who are you?" Tessa sensed magic emanating from the woman, and it matched the barrier outside. It didn't take Einstein to figure out she was the one who'd erected it.

"My name is Delia."

Well, one question answered. "What are you?" She sensed witch, but this woman was something more.

"I'm a Vai." She cocked her head. "I can see you've no idea what that is. My mother was a witch and my father a demon. That's why you didn't recognize the magic in the barrier."

Tessa pinched the bridge of her nose. "So you've been watching me this entire time. Why am I a prisoner here?"

"Because the cat has a jealous streak and a wish to claim the Jinn, Crone, for herself. Fortunately for you, her human side doesn't want you harmed, therefore you'll live out your life here."

There was that panic again. "You can't be serious. Why would you do this to me? I'm a witch." Delia had to realize that Tessa could live a few hundred years. The pit in her stomach grew.

"It's nothing personal, only a matter of money. I will see to your needs."

Panic turned to irritation. "My needs? My needs are to leave here and go home."

Delia moved about the room and picked at the back of a heavy leather chair. "The only way Ares might consider letting you leave is with Zadicus." Her green gaze lifted to catch Tessa's. "Even she realizes that isn't a good relationship."

"Relationship?" Tessa ran her fingers through her hair. "He wants to steal my magic, allow some stranger to rape me until I become pregnant, and give birth to a daughter who'll have the same fate."

"Exactly why you'd be better to stay here." The Vai leaned in with a twinkle in her eye. "I could even summon you a sex demon to help with those lonely nights. There's no reason you can't have a nice life here. You just can't have Crone."

"What? No! I don't want a sex demon or to spend my entire life here." She fisted her hands. "I want to go home and forget all of this."

"You admit you don't want the Jinn either?"

Tessa couldn't believe she was actually having this conversation. Did she want the Jinn... Seriously? Truth be told, said Jinn did belong to her, and she'd be within her right to claim him as her mate. Did she want a man who didn't desire her? He'd likely welcome Ares as his mate since apparently he'd already welcomed her to his bed.

"Why does Ares even think I want Crone?"

Delia glided across the room. "Apparently you two created quite a scene on the beach earlier."

"That was a ruse to trap Zadicus," Tessa scoffed. *But you freaking liked it.* Of course she liked it, she wasn't dead for crying out loud. And yes, she did need Crone to take her virginity so she could get Tara's magic back. "Well hell. I had no idea Ares was in love with him."

The witch laughed. "Oh she doesn't love him. She only wants to claim him as her mate. He rescued her, and she feels he'd be a good provider for her children."

Tessa smacked her palm to her forehead, closed her eyes, and sighed. "Listen, I propose a plan." She couldn't believe she was about to do this. "I only needed to sleep with Crone to gain my Nana's power back. However, there is a different spell that can be cast that allows me to break the curse. Crone was collecting the items needed from Zadicus so we could do that. Since I was abducted by Ares, I'm not even sure if he was successful." She wrung her hands. "Hell, are the Jinn okay?"

"They're fine, but Zadicus escaped. I can't say if Crone collected what you needed. Tell me more about this spell."

Tessa repeated what she'd told Crone earlier. Delia showed no emotion, so Tessa was unsure what the witch...demon was thinking. "You said earlier, this was about money. How much to get you to help me? I have a brick of gold, and it's yours if you help me at least break the spell." She'd have to worry later about a revengeful warlock coming after her.

"I'll admit I'm intrigued. If you promise to stake no claim on Crone, I'll speak to Ares. I'm sure I can get her to agree."

"I promise. Witch's honor." *May the ancestors protect me from this lie.* She wanted her grandmother's power back, and if she had to risk starting a bond with Crone by sleeping with him to get it then that's what she'd do.

CHAPTER EIGHT

Zadicus cursed while Khrom pulled bits of sand from his skin. "Fucking wretched Jinn. I will wipe out the lot of them. Ow!" He jerked and flashed his apprentice an evil glare.

"Sorry." Khrom set aside the tweezers and blotted blood with a damp cloth.

Zadicus mumbled under his breath. "Tell me what have you learned about this Crone."

"His family is the strongest among the Jinn. His older brother only recently came back into the family fold." Khrom tossed the cloth back into the bowl of water and rose from his seat to stoke the fire. "It seems he had been cursed by an angry genie who stripped his magic and banned him to earth."

The warlock stroked his short beard. "How did he break the curse?"

Khrom looked back from poking the fire. "A woman. Her name is Makayla, and it seems she destroyed the genie."

Zadicus's heart rate increased. "Did he mate with this female?"

"She is his *vetemba,* and it seems Crone is smitten with his new sister-in-law, as well as being close to his brothers."

Zadicus experienced a rush of power. A *vetemba* was a Jinn's other half. A rare female destined to be one with the Jinn and help increase his power. It was some wonderful lovey-dovey match, and the thought made the warlock ill. He believed in more of a "take what you want" approach. However, this made his life much easier. "Looks like we've found the perfect weakness." Zadicus moved to a shimmering pool of water so clear he could see the rocks fifty feet below. Closing his eyes, he waved his hand over the top and chanted a locating spell. When he opened them, the water had transformed into a window revealing a dark-haired woman on the other side. Zadicus had to admit, her beauty was astounding, and he would take pleasure in having her company.

"Come, Khrom. I'll need your power so I may break through their barrier." The demon stepped beside him and they joined hands, chanting until a portal opened, and Zadicus was able to show himself.

"Jinn queen," he whispered.

Makayla startled and looked up from the papers on her desk. "Who are you?"

The warlock made sure to put on his best demeanor. "I'm a friend. Your mate and brother are in trouble. You must come quickly."

She rose from her seat so fast the chair fell backwards. "Armand?" There was concern in her voice. "Is he hurt?"

"He's trapped and I need your help to free them both. My magic isn't strong enough, so he told me to summon you."

She stepped around her desk then stopped. "Why does he not summon me himself?"

Damn bitch. Very well. Zadicus projected his magic until he was able to imitate Armand's faint voice and commanded it to speak her name.

"Kayla."

"He's weak. You must hurry," Zadicus urged.

The Jinn queen stepped closer to his portal, still hesitant. "Armand?"

"Kayla, help me."

She moved closer, but Zadicus could tell she was weary. One more step and he'd have her. "Are you not going to help your husband?"

Another step and he sent out his black magic and sucked her in, slamming the portal shut behind her. His hysterical laughter filled the chamber. "Females are weak, and males even weaker, when they are in love. Always remember Khrom, find your enemies true love, and you will win the war every time." He flung his cape aside and strode down the stone stairs to the dungeon where the female would no doubt be spitting obscenities. As he rounded the corner, he could hear her ear-splitting curses and couldn't help but laugh.

"Such a foul mouth for a lady." He stopped in front of her cell and she came at the bars with the force of a Hell cat.

"Let me out," she whispered in such a calm tone it almost made him shiver.

"Perhaps if you behave, I'll send you home once I get what I want."

"And what is that?" she spat.

"Crone has taken something that belongs to me. I mean to have her back, and you'll be my ticket to getting just that."

She crossed her arms and lifted her chin. "You must be the asshole harassing Tessa."

He chuckled. "I am."

Her gaze narrowed, and the darks of her eyes lit with fire. "You realize you just declared war between the Jinn and warlocks. If you release me quickly, they will never know I'm missing."

He wrapped his fingers around the bars. "I love war. You should have stayed a human, it would have been much safer than stepping into a world of immortals. Warlocks are superior."

She snorted. "Apparently you're an idiot. I'm the queen of two houses. You'll have the entire Jinn nation on your ass like a snake on a rat."

"You are a saucy wench."

She grinned. "I've learned from the best. My brother-in-law, Crone."

Armand and Lazaro both sat impatiently, drumming their fingers on the table. Crone paced until his father, Efrain, flashed into the room.

"Sorry I'm late. I sent feelers out to locate the girl."

Crone turned and tried to control his anger. "That girl…" He swallowed and gulped in a deep breath. "Fuck."

Armand jumped to his feet. "Tessa is Crone's *vetemba*."

"Shit," Efrain replied. "When did you realize this?"

"When she went missing." He scraped his fingers over his scalp. "Oh fuck, probably when I kissed her. I don't know. All I do know is I have to find her." Was that panic in his voice? He'd never panicked in his entire life. No, that wasn't right. He'd panicked when Morden had brought Tara into the room so many years ago. He panicked again when she'd died in his arms.

How fucking messed up was his life? His other half was the granddaughter of the woman he'd failed to save. He couldn't have a real relationship with her without that memory surfacing, yet his heart broke at the thought of her in harm's way. His body burned for her and his soul. It screamed to wipe out the entire warlock nation.

Power electrified the air and a mirror portal opened with Zadicus's ugly mug in plain view. Crone readied himself, as did the other males in the room.

"Figures you'd not have enough balls to open a real portal," Crone stated. With a mirror, it only allowed viewing and not jumping to the other side. *Bastard.*

Zadicus laughed. "My balls are quite large. Matter of fact, I'm delighted to see the family together." The warlock touched his index finger to his chin. "Oh, wait… I believe there is a member missing." The mirror shifted from viewing Zadicus to…

Armand ran for the portal. "You son of a bitch!" Crone, Lazaro, and Efrain stepped in behind the distraught Jinn.

"Kayla, baby, tell me you're okay." Armand was as pale as a ghost and Crone's anger ignited further. He wouldn't kill Zadicus. Instead, he'd invent the vilest torture he could think of, and right now his imagination was pretty fucking active.

"I'm fine. Don't give in to his demands." Makayla wrapped her fingers around the bars.

"What the fuck does he want?" Crone growled.

"He wants Tessa in exchange for me."

Armand began to speak, but their father grabbed his shoulders and hushed his son.

"What are your terms?" Efrain asked, keeping a firm grip on Armand and casting a glance to his other sons. Crone and his brother's knew to let the elder handle the negotiations.

"Simple. You have forty-eight hours to bring the witch. Bring her to Armand's Spanish home and we will make the exchange," Zadicus demanded and snapped the mirror portal shut.

Armand jerked free of his father's grip, and Crone nearly fell to his knees. "If he doesn't have Tessa then where the hell is she?"

Efrain held his hands up. "Let's all keep our heads and come up with a plan."

"Easy for you to say, father." Armand flexed his fingers. "My wife is in the hands of that warlock, and the gods only know where Crone's female is."

Crone couldn't even speak. He had no idea where Tessa could have gone. "I'm going to her apartment to look for her. Maybe she went back home while we were fighting Zadicus." He doubted it but had to search.

"Good idea." Efrain nodded. "We'll all head back to my home and come up with a plan. Meet us there as soon as you can."

The others left and Crone opened a portal to Tessa's small apartment. When he entered, the place was dark and still in shambles from his earlier encounter with the warlock. "Tessa?" He knew she wasn't here and hadn't been since he'd taken here away. Her scent was too weak. He waved his hand and turned on the lights. The sight of broken furniture and charred bits turned his stomach. With a snap, he had the room back to its original clean and unbroken state. Moving down the tiny hall, he came across the only bedroom in the apartment.

He stepped inside.

His gaze darted from one side to the other and took stock of everything in the room. A small bed on one side and a three-drawer dresser on the other. The single door he assumed led to a closet. He shook his head. The witch lived like a pauper. In three strides, he was to the dresser, pulling open the first drawer. Not what he expected. He lifted the unsightly white undies from their resting place.

"My mate will not wear such...granny panties." He flicked the unappealing dainties to the floor and imagined Tessa wearing silk and lace in brilliant jewel toned colors against her skin. He continued to the next drawer and found a few T-shirts and a couple pairs of shorts. With disgust, he walked to the closet and flung it open. What he was looking for he had no clue, but his gut said he'd find it.

The closet provided little: only a few pairs of shoes, some jeans, and a jacket or two. With a huff, he left the bedroom and stormed into the bathroom. Gardenias filled the tiny room, and he noted the bottle of shampoo in the shower. He closed his eyes and let the aroma of her linger over him, remembered what it was like to kiss her and have her heat scorching his skin. Determination settled across him and he opened his eyes, his gaze landing on a hairbrush.

"There you are." He grabbed it and flashed to his father's house. Once there, he strode into the study where the others were gathered around a stack of books.

"What are you looking for?" Crone asked.

Armand raised his head to peer over the large leather book he was holding. "Anything. What's with the hair brush?"

"Having a piece of Tessa might help me find her. Did you try connecting with Kayla?" Crone moved to stand beside his father.

"I tried and of course the bastard has her blocked. I'm searching for any kind of spell, folk lore, or old legend that might help me get to her."

"Damn." Crone turned to his father. "I need a witch to perform the bonding."

"Son, are you certain?"

Lazaro jumped to his feet and grabbed Crone by the arm. "Excuse us while I speak to my brother alone." He flashed them from the study to the gardens outside. "Are you fucking crazy?"

Crone's heart pounded as his feet made contact with the stone walkway. "She belongs to me."

His brother folded his arms. "I'm aware. However, it seems I must remind you of two things."

"Don't even go there," Crone spat.

"Or what?" Lazaro unfolded his arms and stepped into Crone's space. His brother dared jab his finger into his chest. "I'm going there, like it or not. First off, you can't even look at her without rehashing the past. How the fuck do you expect to have a relationship with her?"

"Step away, brother." Crone snarled.

Lazaro jabbed again. "Fuck you. Even if you succeed in bonding her to you, you're doing it without her consent. She's already been cursed and bonded to a warlock. How do you think this will make her feel?"

"I'm aware of the consequences and I'll deal." He was painfully conscious of what it all meant. With time, he was certain he could get over the ordeal with Tara and come to terms. But Lazaro was right. Performing the ritual would bond him to Tessa, and she could end up hating him for it. "Besides, it may save her. If Zadicus manages to get his hands on her, he'll quickly find out she's taken."

The younger Jinn shook his head. "Shit, Crone. You're going to ride everything on the hopes that your bond will trump the curse?"

"That's exactly what I'm doing." The chances were pretty good that Zadicus wouldn't be able to touch her. Nor would any other man for that fact, and for some reason that alone made his chest puff out. Of course, it wouldn't protect her from Zadicus's wrath when he found out.

Lazaro stepped back. "I'm only trying to save you from a world of pain. We don't even know for sure if you'll be able to connect with her once the bond is completed. Look at Armand, he can't get to Kayla and their love knows no bounds. Not to mention how will it affect you if she decides to walk away."

Crone lifted the brown plastic brush that held Tessa's strands of hair and stared at it. "I know it's a long shot and realize it's crazy, but I have to do something." He met his brothers blue eyes. "The longing I have for her. The ache I feel in my heart is real, and I cannot explain it.

I don't even fully understand how, after one brief moment...a stolen kiss on the beach could make me feel so crazed, but it does."

His brother sighed. "And that is why I'm afraid she will break your heart. Our species, as a whole, bonds deeply with their mate. I'm not sure that witches, especially one forced into a relationship, feel the same. However, I will stand behind you no matter what." Lazaro pulled Crone into an embrace and slapped him on the back. "Come, let's find your mate."

CHAPTER NINE

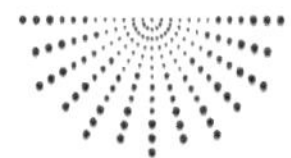

essa could hardly wait until the witch, Delia, was gone. After she was sure the she-devil had departed, she ran to the main room where a fire crackled in the large fireplace. If memory served her correctly, and it usually didn't, she could try to connect with Crone. All she had to do was cast the right spell.

She snorted. "When have I ever worked a spell correctly?" Several times. Okay, maybe a couple? More like once or twice if she were lucky. This time, however, her life depended on it.

Her gut twisted. If she failed, she would be stuck here forever. She shivered and rubbed her arms. It wasn't the chill that got to her but fear. She wasn't so stupid to realize that Delia was much more powerful than her. She looked up to the ceiling.

"May the ancestors be with me and help guide my magic." She knelt on the warm stone floor in front of the fire and rubbed her palms together. Closing her eyes, she pulled up Crone's face, imagined they were on the beach together, and he was kissing her. Butterflies filled her stomach and desire her sex.

"*Phasse dydi, craraj. Ephufus ecimukius, shefar, ekrashick, korar, fraru, nablikien. Brypa nopakar, obreyiria, frosa. Cive fralia, hog, precryu, okrak, vadus.*"

Power stirred, and she was afraid to open her eyes. Finally summoning her courage, she peered through barely open lids. Nothing. She rose to her feet when something caused her skin to prickle. Turning, she nearly jumped into the fire.

"Umm, you're not Crone."

The man standing there, wearing only a pair of jeans, smiled. "I can be whoever you wish, mistress. My name's Darsam, but I'll answer to Crone."

Shit, shitty, shit, shit! She'd managed to summon a sex demon. Well, what had she expected when she was busy thinking of Crone and sex? "Look. Summoning you was a mistake. I meant for someone else." Though she did have to admit, if not in such a predicament, he was hotter than Hell. Pun intended. Caramel-colored hair, tied back with a piece of leather, accentuated his smoldering golden eyes. Bronzed skin covered a muscular body that was made for pleasuring a woman and when her gaze dropped lower, there was no mistaking the enormous bulge in his pants. He was all kinds of yummy, but truth be told she only wanted Crone. Not because he was the one who could give back her Nana's power, hence helping her break the curse, she simply wanted him. No, she craved him like a woman craved chocolate. There would be nothing stopping her until she was satisfied.

He took a step toward her. She skirted to the other side of the sofa.

"Since I'm the one who's here, we could have some fun." Another step.

"Told you, not interested."

"I can make you interested. I promise I can do the most delightful things and have you coming in seconds." Two steps.

Tessa darted across the room. This was a fine mess she'd gotten herself into and with no idea how to get out of it. Once summoned, a sex demon was bound to please his master or in this case his mistress. Unless she could send him back––which was about as likely as connecting with Crone––she'd be in a heap of trouble. No locked door would keep the demon away. Time to try and fix this mess.

"Brypa nopakar, obreyiria, frosa. Cive fralia, hog, precryu, okrak, vadus. Phasse dydi, craraj. Ephufus ecimukius, shefar, ekrashick, korar, fraru, nablikien."

Damn, he was still there. What had she done?

BAAAAAA.

She felt her jaw unhinge as she spun around. "Oh mother... Son of a... Shit!"

"Ohh, how cute. A little goat," Darsam stated.

She cast a sideways glare. "Shut it."

The demon laughed, and oh how she wanted to punch something, but she wasn't sure what. Maybe she'd start with the warlock who started this mess then move on to Crone. Though she was unsure why she wanted to hit him. Maybe it was because he stirred desires in her she hadn't been prepared for, and the fact he was likely sleeping with that damn cat!

"What the hell did I expect?"

Darsam stared at her from the chair he'd planted himself in. "If I may make an observation."

"No."

"Well too bad." He stifled a yawn, looking bored as ever. "Seems you've lost your heart to another man. Perhaps his name is Crone?"

Tessa snorted. "You've been here what, all of ten minutes?"

"I'm an observant demon. First off, a female never refuses me unless there's another man. I can also assume since you were looking for a man named Crone when you summoned me that he must be the one who has stolen your heart."

She crossed her arms and began to pace. "You don't know shit. Crone is the Jinn who was supposed to protect me, yet here I am. Stuck in this"--she waved her hands around--"damn castle. I have a warlock who wants my power."

Darsam raised a brow. "Really? Why would he want that? Seems you have the power of a child, not yet fully developed."

The demon had no idea how correct he was. Tessa plopped into a chair and dropped her head into her hands. "I'm one hot mess." She lifted her head, ready to spill to the man across from her. Hell, she might as well make use of his company. "I was cursed at birth to be taken by a warlock. He will strip my power, and then hand me over to a man of his choosing to father a daughter so the curse can continue. When he's had his fill of me, he will kill me."

"Damn. So how does this Crone fit into the picture?"

She gazed into the fire and watched the flames perform an erotic dance. Every time she thought of the Jinn, her body became as ignited as those flames. "My grandmother was also plagued by this same curse. Crone was a slave to the warlock, and he tried to save her life. On her last breath, she gave him what power she had left and called to the ancestors to grant him a mate. I am that mate. However, I've no intention of breaking the curse from the warlock then becoming mated to a Jinn. It would be like jumping from the caldron into the fire." Why was she trying so hard to convince herself it wasn't what she wanted?

The demon leaned closer. "This story gets more interesting. A real fairy tale. So how did you end up here?"

"A tiger shifter who wants my mate for herself." There was that anger again, bubbling to the surface like hot lava, and oh how she'd like to burn that bitch.

"So, you say you don't want to accept your mate. So why do you care if the cat has him?"

She jumped to her feet. "I'm going to bed." She headed out of the room, the demon chuckling behind her. Yeah, her life was freaking hysterical.

Tessa tossed and turned all night, sleep evaded her as Darsam's words repeated in her mind. Why did she care so much if Ares had Crone? She sat up and swung her feet to the cold floor. Last night she'd stumbled across this room. Apparently laid out for her. The dresser and closet held clothes exactly her size.

How convenient.

She walked to the vanity and sat on the stool, staring at her reflection in the mirror. Darkness circled her eyes and her skin was more pale than usual. Her hair, a mass of waves, looked like it hadn't seen a brush in weeks. What would Crone see in her anyway? He'd likely be pissed to discover his chosen was a witch who couldn't cast a spell to save her life and certainly was not even close to Ares sex appeal. The cat was stunning in both forms. Tessa wondered if he was kissing her at this very moment. Was he making love to her? She was sure Ares had gotten exactly what she wanted. Tessa looked down and her hands were shaking. She picked up the vase of flowers sitting on the vanity and threw them at the mirror. Her reflection cracked into tiny pieces.

The door flung open. "Are you...oh. You know that's seven years of bad luck." Darsam stated the obvious.

"Only if you believe in mortal superstitions. Besides, could my luck get any worse?" As if on cue to remind her of how inept she was, the goat entered and began nibbling the flowers that were strewn across the room. She jumped up and shooed the animal away. "Don't eat those, there's broken glass everywhere." No sooner had the words spilled from her mouth than her foot landed right on a shard, digging into her heel.

"Oooowww. Holy mother of..." She hobbled, blood dripping, when she was suddenly scooped up and laid on the bed.

"You really are one hot mess," Darsam noted as he examined her foot.

Tessa flopped back on the pillow, disgusted with herself. "Can you pull it out?" A shadow moved behind the demon. "Umm, what's that?"

"Demon! Step away from the witch."

Crone.

Darsam straightened and stepped aside so Tessa could see. A mirror portal was open and Crone's angry face stared back at her. So, he'd been busy sleeping with the cat and now he thought to be angry with her?

"I stepped on some glass, and he was trying to help." She pushed herself up to rest on her elbows.

"Clearly. If you wanted to get away with the demon, you only had to tell me. We've wasted a lot of time looking for you."

She searched for a snappy comeback, but realized how things looked. "Crone, I'm trapped and umm, I can explain. I was trying to connect with you." She picked at the blanket, suddenly caring that he knew she'd not slept with the demon.

"I see. So..."

BAAAAAA.

Both dark brows shot up. "Is that a goat?"

"Sorta. Yes." She cast her gaze downward.

"Good lord woman. What is it with you and farm animals?"

Tessa straightened and lifted her chin. "I happen to like farm animals."

He shook his head. "For the love of the gods, don't perform any more witchcraft. Demon, step closer." Darsam did as commanded until he stood directly in front of the mirror portal. "Good. Now I understand your situation. Unless you'd like to be skinned alive and have your man junk spread from one side of the universe to the other, I suggest you refrain from touching the witch until I get there. Understood?"

The demon nodded. "I'd like to keep my body parts intact, thank you."

"Crone? I've no idea where I am, but Ares is behind this. She did say something about her family home." She hated to tell him the shifter was responsible, but he needed to know. Okay, maybe a tiny part of her was more than thrilled to throw that bitch under the bus.

"Know this, witch. You're mine and I'm coming to get you." The portal slammed shut.

"I'd say you've just been claimed," Darsam stated from a safe distance.

"Oh my."

Crone slammed the portal shut before he totally lost his cool. His father came up behind him and squeezed his shoulders.

"Son, I'm sure there's a logical explanation for a sex demon being in her company."

"I'm sure there is." His witch couldn't cast her way out of a paper bag. Crone took in a slow, deep breath to help ease his anger. *His witch.* He had no claim on Tessa, even though he'd managed to find a witch who'd been willing to call upon their ancestors. After some herbs were burned along with chants, he had willingly accepted her as his mate. Once bonded, he had connected with her only to find her with another man. "We need to get her out of there, and then I'll deal with Ares."

"Would it be easier to simply ask Ares what's going on and have her take you to Tessa?" Armand asked. Crone understood his brother was itching to get his wife back, and the thought of wasting time and energy on a rescue only made him more restless.

"You're right. The rest of you concentrate on getting Kayla home, and I'll deal with this."

"As you wish, but call us if you need help," Lazaro replied.

Crone shifted to smoke and headed for his own home, hoping Ares would be there. He found it difficult to comprehend why she would harm Tessa. When he arrived, he was relieved to see the tiger shifter sitting on the couch flipping through a magazine.

"Crone, I was getting worried about you."

"Ares. We need to talk." He fought to control his anger. She'd lied to him about Tessa's whereabouts, but if he scared her then she'd likely flee.

She closed her magazine and placed it on the table. "Okay."

He refused to sit, too uptight to keep still. "Where have you hidden Tessa?" So much for subtlety.

She chewed her bottom lip, a good indicator she was about to lie. "I don't know what you mean. I thought the warlock took her."

He moved to tower over her. "Ares, I've treated you like a sister. Don't continue your deceit. I've spoken to Tessa, and I know you have her hidden. Where and why?"

She averted her gaze. "She isn't a good match for you."

Every muscle coiled tight. "She is my *vetemba.*" He watched as Ares shoulders sank. She looked like the frightened girl he had rescued long ago.

"I'm so sorry. You know I'd never intentionally hurt you."

"Damn it, Ares." He began to relax. "What were you thinking?"

"I had hoped we could mate."

He dropped to his knees in front of her. "Shit. Did I... I'm so sorry if I did something to make you believe we'd ever be more than friends." He tried to flip though his memories and came up with nothing.

"No, of course not. You've always treated me like a sister. I just"--she cast her gaze to her lap, a tear landed on her hand--"I'm so sorry." Suddenly she was gone.

"Ares?" Crone jumped to his feet panic beating him like a wild stallion. "Damn it, Ares come back here!"

Silence greeted him, but then he noticed a piece of paper where she'd sat. He snatched it up and unfolded it. A map. This was where he'd find his mate. Crone clapped his palms together and rubbed until the room filled with several Rabbons, small demons that stood about three feet high. Their bodies were covered with light green skin, pointed ears topped their head, and large black eyes made their round faces cuter than hell. Until they smiled and showed two rows of razor sharp teeth. The demons were normally harmless if their bellies were kept full, at least until Crone commanded them to show no mercy. They'd been known to devour their victims in a most grisly way.

"You!" He pointed to the group on his right. "Patrol the area and if you even smell that tiger I want to know immediately." To the others. "Split up. I want that fucking warlock found above all else."

The demons chattered in a language only Crone understood and took off to obey his command. There were some benefits to having pet demons. Now to go collect his mate.

CHAPTER TEN

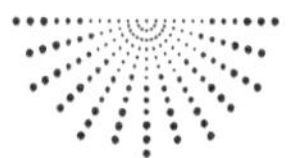

Tessa paced nervously, her flip-flops smacking the tile floor. Darsam watched her with an intent gaze. Or more like a hungry one. She wasn't sure how much longer the demon could hold out. After all, he required sex to stay alive. Then there were Crone's words. What exactly did he mean by them?

A flash of light and Crone stood beside her. "Demon, time for you to go back home." Crone snapped his fingers and Darsam vanished. Damn, she wished just once her magic would work so well.

"I'm happy you're here. I wasn't exactly thrilled with spending my life trapped in this castle. Not to be pushy or anything, but can we go now?" Tessa shifted nervously.

"Care to tell me how you ended up here with a sex demon?" His tone accusatory.

"Who are you to be so angry? I told you, your little cat whore brought me here and left me trapped." Oh, she had not meant for that to be spoken out loud. *Damn it!* Crone flashed her the look that said he was pissed. *Suck it up asshat.* She was beyond angry.

"I'm not the one who had to conjure a sex demon. I mean you've been missing all of what... A day?" He stepped closer to her.

76

Tessa didn't budge. "Perhaps, but at least it wasn't my lover who locked you away in this hole."

BAAAAAA. The goat mocked them both.

"Oh, for all that's holy in the magical realm. Send that damn thing back where it came from," he snarled.

She narrowed her gaze and slapped her hands on her hips. "What is your aversion to animals?"

"I happen to like animals. I'm simply more of an exotic animal man versus farm creatures."

Oh that did it. All Tessa could see was Crone…her Jinn, in bed with that cat. She clenched her jaw, pissed at him, and even more so at herself for giving a shit who he slept with. She lashed out, her hand making contact with his cheek. The sound rang through the quiet air. Even the goat dared not make a sound. Crone's eyes widened briefly before his brows shot down into a V.

"Listen up little witch." He stepped forward, and she scooted back. Hadn't she done this earlier? Except her pursuer had been a demon in lust, now she faced an angry Jinn.

He countered. She turned and ran, skirted around a table, and laughed that she'd managed not to trip over the damn thing. When she looked behind her, Crone was nowhere to be found, and suddenly she hit a hard wall of muscle.

Oh shit.

Strong arms snaked around her and crushed her to a warm body. She didn't have to look to know Crone had her. Tessa tipped her head back and stared into a blue pool of desire. His mouth came down on hers, and she tried to struggle. When he swiped his tongue across her lips, she melted and opened for his tongue to dart inside and dance with hers. Fire ignited and her knees weakened. Everything else was blocked out except for her pounding pulse. Tessa had been kissed before but never like this. This man consumed her.

Shit! She came to her senses and kneed him in his man junk. He howled and released her. Bending over, he glared a death threat.

"Are you trying to help Zadicus find me?" She fought to bring her breathing back to normal. Damn, she missed his warmth already and hell if her body wasn't twisted into a sexual knot. She no longer cared about herself; her worry was for his safety.

He straightened. "Shoving your knee into my groin was not the way to get my attention."

"Oh I don't know. Worked didn't it?" She batted her lashes.

"Saucy wench."

"Besides, I'm sure Ares wouldn't be very happy with you, cheating on her." The mention of that woman's name set her teeth on edge.

He cocked his head. "How do you propose I cheat on a woman I have no relationship with?"

Now she felt kinda bad for the cat. "You're an ass." Even friends with benefits deserved some respect. He raked a hand through his hair. His long, thick black hair that made her jealous of said hand.

"I thought we'd already established I was an ass. Come up with something better next time."

She sighed. "Did you get the items needed to help me break the curse?" Change of subject was always good.

"Two out of three. But there's another problem," he stated.

"What's that?"

"Zadicus is holding my sister-in-law hostage."

Tessa slapped her hand over her mouth. "Oh no," she mumbled.

"That's not all."

Dropping her hand. "There's more?"

"As my mate..."

She let her jaw drop.

"Yes, I know. In order to protect you, I've bonded to you. Zadicus can no longer claim your virginity."

She wanted to ask questions, had a million of them, but they would have to wait. Right now, the queen's safe return outweighed everything.

For the love of the gods, this witch would be his undoing. At least-- for the moment--she was safe, and now he could focus on his other duties. Hopefully, there would be good news when they returned home.

"Oh, my god. Queen Makayla?" Tessa's voice was laced with concern.

"Yes. So can we go now?"

"Of course. I'm so sorry." She smoothed her hair, and he wanted to slide his fingers through it, grab a handful, and pull her head back while he kissed the hell out of her. It would be worth a knee in the balls to taste her again.

"Give me your hand," he said. She hesitated only for a moment before slipping her hand in his.

"What about the goat?" She looked back, and he flicked his other wrist, sending the animal back to its farm before he pulled Tessa through the portal and back to his father's home. Once on the other side, he released his grip, hating to lose her warmth.

All the men looked up from the books they had their noses buried in. Lazaro set his aside. "I'm glad to see you safe, Tessa."

"I'm glad to be back. I understand Zadicus has the queen?"

"Yes. Sorry, my manners are lacking, but I can't think of anything except my wife at the moment." Crone caught the note of panic in Armand's voice and fully understood.

"What can I do to help?" Tessa inquired. "And why did he take the queen?" Suddenly her eyes widened. "It's because of me."

"It's because the warlock is an asshole," Crone ground out.

"He wants to make an exchange, you for her," Armand shot back, and Crone gave him an *I'll kill you later* glare.

"Then that's what we do." Tessa approached Armand. "What are the logistics? He must have indicated how he wanted to swap."

The thought of his mate turning herself over to Zadicus...not in his fucking lifetime. There had to be another solution. "When Hell freezes over, and as far as I know that will never happen."

She faced him, all full of fire, and he was ready to battle with her. He'd lock her in the dungeon if it kept her from harm. Actually, the thought of her chained to the wall, helpless and at his disposal, caused his cock to stir. Damn, what a sight she'd make naked and ready for him.

Shit. Shake that vision free right now.

"Crone's right. I'll not risk his mate to save my own. We'll come up with a plan." Armand went back to flipping through the pages of text.

"I have my minions on the search." Crone started to walk toward the wall of books when Tessa stepped in front of him.

"You have no say over what I do, and what's with all this mate stuff?" Golden embers smoldered in her dark eyes. Time to battle.

"Don't test me. You will lose." He surprised himself at his calm demeanor. Tessa looked around and noted the other men staring at her. No doubt, they too were waiting for the battle.

"Can we go somewhere more private?" she pleaded, and Crone was ready to drag her off to a remote area when his father yelled out.

"I found it!" Everyone turned to the elder Jinn.

"What did you find?" Armand jumped up to move next to his father.

Tessa leaned closer to Crone. "Who's that?"

"Our father. Sorry, I was remiss with the introductions."

"There are more important things going on," she whispered. "Like what did your father find?"

Efrain looked up from the scroll he had rolled out on the table. "An old legend. I didn't want to mention it until I was certain I could locate it." He pointed and Armand looked over his shoulder.

"What is it, father?" Crone's brother asked.

"There is an old legend of a king who went missing. His people were so distraught they combined their power to help locate him."

Crone moved closer, he sensed Tessa right behind him. "Father, I've never heard of this legend." He knew that many of these stories were folklore, tales to send children to sleep at night.

"It's very old and not something spoken about. It was believed it best to keep this power a secret, and I nearly forgot about it myself." The elder pointed to the scroll. "It's also considered dark magic and can produce unwanted side effects."

"Just spill," Armand growled. Crone felt for his older brother, knew how crazed he'd been wondering what had happened to Tessa.

"The legend states that any royal member of a house can be summoned by their people. They only need to call upon their powers and combine them together. The more Jinn, the better the chance of success. The downfall? It's black magic, no one knows what doorway it will open."

"I don't give two shits if it opens a door directly to the devil's piss pot. What do we need to do?" Armand asked, his muscles coiled tight and ready to pounce at any second. Crone couldn't remember the last time he'd witnessed his older brother ready to kill anything that twitched.

"Gather as many people from Kayla's house as possible, and yours too. Everyone meet in the temple. At midnight we call upon the darkness and attempt to find your wife."

Tessa looked to Crone. "What can I do?"

Efrain approached as Armand and Lazaro disappeared. "I'm sorry that things are crazy right now. As soon as we get the queen back, you and I will get better acquainted."

"Why are you sorry? I'm the cause of all this mess." So many things had gone bad, and if she'd just left well enough alone and submitted to Zadicus, the queen wouldn't be in danger. None of them, with the exception of herself, would have had to worry. How selfish she'd been in thinking she could break the curse.

Efrain shoved Crone aside and placed a strong arm around her shoulder. "Nonsense." He eyed his son. "Give us a few minutes." Crone started to object. "I'm not asking."

"Fine." He vanished.

"Wow. No smart ass remark? I'm impressed," Tessa snorted.

"He knows to pick his battles. You realize he only has your best interest at heart?" The older Jinn asked.

Tessa thought for a moment. "Yes. Even though he can be arrogant as hell, I sense the kindness in him." Efrain gave her a squeeze before releasing her. "I suspect he carries a large amount of guilt for the death of my Nana." And for that her heart ached.

"You would be correct, and perhaps you can help him finally let it go."

"I'm not sure what I can do other than assure him he bears no responsibility."

"That would be a start, and as his *vetemba*, it would hold value."

Tessa tried to keep her features schooled, but knew she failed. "Does everyone know?"

"Yes. He told us when he realized you were missing. I get the feeling you're not pleased by this news? May I ask how long you've known?"

Did she dare tell him? Yes, the elder Jinn made her feel comfortable, as if he would never judge her. She wanted to confide in him. "Since I was a child. My mother told me that Nana gave Crone her power and asked the ancestors to grant him a mate on her dying breath." She searched his face for any indication of how he felt about this bit of news but saw nothing. Like father, like son. "My mother encouraged me to seek Crone out. Not only would I be able to get Nana's power back, which would help me break our curse, she wanted me to find happiness."

He seemed to contemplate for a moment before speaking. "So what is it you want from my son?"

Now, there was the million-dollar question. "I want Nana's power and to break the curse. In the beginning, that was all I wanted. Now... I'm not so sure."

"I understand. You were not expecting the attraction you feel. Being his *vetemba* isn't something you'll be able to walk away from easily. I only ask that you don't make any rash decisions that you'll later regret." He smiled. "I don't mind admitting I'd love to welcome you into the family, but enough. Crone is probably beside himself waiting for us to finish." Efrain headed for the high archway that led out of the library, and Tessa was left to wonder what she was going to do about this whole mess.

CHAPTER ELEVEN

The second Crone saw his father leave the library, he made a mad dash back into the room. Being separated from Tessa caused him severe anxiety and made his mood even fouler. He was in a no-win situation. The only thing that made up for it was the fact that his bond now superseded Zadicus's. The warlock couldn't take her virginity, or so the witch who had performed the bonding had promised. However, that alone didn't protect her.

"Did you and my father have a nice chat?"

Tessa jumped. Apparently not hearing him enter the room, she'd been busy looking at the wall of books. "It was fine. He's a nice man."

He nearly laughed. Yes, Efrain was a good man, but she'd never seen him when someone had crossed him. The older Jinn's bad side was not a place to be. "I hold a great deal of respect for my father."

Her smile faded. "You are lucky, Crone. To have a father who cares about you."

It had never occurred to him what her childhood must have been like. Fathered by a man who had been chosen for nothing more than breeding. Tessa's mother forced to conceive and bear a child with no love in her life. He suddenly felt ill and wanted to break free. Go to the one place that always gave him comfort. He reached for her hand and entwined his fingers with hers.

"Let's go someplace more peaceful until we are needed later." He opened a portal and took them back to his private beach. Darkness had colored the sky an inky black, but the moon was full and bright. Waves crashed on the sand and lulled him into a peaceful state of mind.

"Wow. Last time I saw this beach there were fireworks of an unnatural kind going on." She stiffened and tried to free her hand from his. He reluctantly released her, sensing she needed some space. "So why bring me back here? To the place where your lover pretended to take me to safety?"

Crone wiped his palm down his face. "Why do you insist Ares is my lover? I've never touched her in that way."

She stepped back. "Don't lie to me. Just because you have apparently figured out I'm your *vetemba* doesn't give you the right to lie to me." Venom dripped from her voice.

"I do not lie. Did Ares tell you something different? I understand what her plans were, and I'm so sorry." He allowed her the space she wanted, but if she backed any further away from him, he'd have to snare her and bring her to a more comfortable distance.

"She said you were friends with benefits." She cocked her head. "Though the witch-demon did say Ares didn't love you."

He let his mouth curl into a grin. "Does that bother you? The fact another woman might love me?"

"Oh, you'd love that, wouldn't you? I bet it empowers you to have women fawning all over you." Was that a snarl? Oh, she was too cute when jealous.

He shrugged. "I'll admit, that in the past it did, but I've since bonded myself to you. Zadicus cannot claim your virginity. Technically, no man can but me." Her jaw dropped. Not the response he was hoping for. *What was I hoping? That she'd jump me right here?* The thought of that caused blood to rush to his nether region.

"Bonded yourself? So the curse is broken?"

He wished it were so. "No. He can still cause you harm, but he cannot take your virginity or force anyone else to do so. They will find themselves impotent in your presence."

"Oh." Suddenly her lips drew into a thin line. "So you've basically taken my free will the same as Zadicus. I'm not allowed to choose what man I desire to sleep with."

Damn that stung, but she was right. "Once we have my sister-in-law back, we'll finish breaking your curse. I'll get the final piece you need from Zadicus before I kill him and all his kind." He realized his fingers had rolled into tight fists.

"So even though you know what I am, you still don't desire me? You bonded to me only to keep another from having me?"

Crone inhaled and the scent of gardenias drifted, mingled with the salty air. Desire her? It was all he could do not to take her right now. Instead, he stepped into her space, pulled her close to him, and brushed his lips across hers. Her body instantly heated and nearly caused him to explode.

"Desire? There isn't a word in any language that describes what I feel, but taking your virginity so you can gain your grandmother's power? Not happening." He slipped his hand under her shirt and rested his palm on her waist. The scent of her arousal wrapped around him and squeezed. Unable to control himself any longer, and not wanting to, he dipped his head and ran his tongue along her neck, upward to her earlobe where he nipped.

"If you want to lose yourself to me *mi amor,* then you're going to have to take what you desire." He felt her shiver, so he slid his hand up her side, enjoying the silky feel of her warm skin against his.

"I-I don't understand what you mean," she whispered.

He continued to kiss her neck, causing her to tip her head to grant him better access. "I don't want this to be about your ancestors' power. This needs to be about your desire for me as your mate. You have total freedom to take this as far as you want." He lifted his head so he could look into her eyes as he brushed his thumb across her nipple. Her eyes closed and lips parted.

Such a beautiful sight.

"Tonight however, I will bring you pleasure right here under the stars, but we will not have sex. I want to give you some relief." *And something to remember me by.* He wanted her mind to be filled with longing for only him.

He grabbed the hem of her tank and pulled the fabric over her head, tossing it to the sand. He could hardly wait to taste her. Wrap his lips around her nipples that were already hardening in the night's breeze. There would be no more waiting. His mouth found what he craved. Sucking on the swollen bud, he swirled his tongue around the areola then across her nipple.

She moaned and pushed into him. Her scent grew stronger. Crone knew he could have her. She'd not protest, but it wasn't how he wanted it and *that* shocked the hell out of him. Instead, his goal for the moment was to make her come so hard she forgot her name.

He guided his right hand to the waistband on her shorts, relieved that it was elastic. Pushing the fabric aside, he slid past her panties and didn't slow his descent until he reached her sex. As he moved his mouth to enjoy the other breast, he slid his fingers through her folds.

"Mmm. So wet," he whispered between nips on her breast. Her breathing increased along with her pulse. She placed her hands on his shoulders and dug her nails into his skin.

Her eyes opened. "Your shirt..."

"Yes, I ditched it so you could touch me if you desired." And apparently, she did. The sensation of her nails spurred him on. He rubbed her juices over her clit while he brought his lips to hers. Pushing his tongue inside and sweeping, he tasted every inch of her mouth. His cock throbbed, but he shoved the sensation to the back of his mind. She pressed her naked breasts against his chest, her hard nipples made the zipper on his jeans even tighter. Before he realized what she was doing, Tessa had unbuttoned his pants and freed his erection. Her hand wrapped around him. Squeezing.

Holy fuck!

Crone kissed her harder, and she responded in kind. He slid a finger into her core, careful to stop when he felt the slightest resistance. Circling his thumb over her clit caused her to shudder, and she pumped him faster. Christ, he wouldn't last long at this rate. The tide washed up and swirled around their feet. The night was calm and perfect for forgetting their troubles, if even for a little while.

He broke their kiss. "Come for me *mi amor*," he spoke against her swollen lips. She surrendered to his command and cried out. Watching his mate orgasm by his hand, as the moonlight caressed her skin, was too much. Pleasure overtook him and he growled out his own release, shooting his come all over her belly. She buried her head into his chest, and he couldn't resist kissing her silky hair. Damn it, how had this woman turned his world upside down?

Tessa's heart rate finally began to slow to normal. She hadn't expected when Crone had brought her out onto the moonlit beach that he'd give her the best orgasm of her life. Yet it had happened, and she wondered why she was even surprised by it. After all, she had found him with the intention of seduction and gaining power. Now? Things had changed. She had been an idiot to underestimate the power of being his mate. Thought she could take what belonged to her and walk away without looking back.

She was torn. She wanted him. Craved him to lick and caress every inch of her body then take her in a mad heat of passion. Her mind was confused. She had been given to two men the moment she was born and sucked in her first breath of air. Bonded to a warlock by a curse and mated to a Jinn at the request of her grandmother. Tara had seen something good in Crone or she wouldn't have asked the ancestors to create such a bond. She looked up at him and knew she had to make a choice. This man had sought a witch to complete his side of the bond to protect her. But was there another reason? He had to know she could still walk away from him, yet he had chosen to do it anyway.

She could break the curse with Zadicus and end his life, so she could live free and go back to her existence. Her magic would likely never obey her commands, so she'd live her life like any other mortal except far longer. Or she could stay with Crone and gain back her Nana's magic. What kind of life would they have together?

He cupped her cheek and seemed to understand her dilemma. "It pains me to say this more than you could ever know. Once Zadicus and his family are dead, I will break my bond with you if that's what you desire. For once in your life, you will be free to make your own choice."

She opened her mouth to speak, but words had become foreign to her.

"Yes, I have the knowledge on how to break our bond but understand this. There will never be another for me. Once you walk away, I will never see you again. Watching you with another man would be like shoving a dagger into my heart."

She swallowed. "I thought Jinn could take another *vetemba*."

"It happens sometimes, but for me it will forever only be you."

She felt tears sting her eyes. He was willing to let her go. Give back her freedom. "I-I don't know what to say."

He stepped back, releasing her, and she found they were both clothed again. "Tell me that you'll become a powerful witch and live a happy life. Once I'm certain of your safety, I know a way to give you back your grandmother's power."

The tears rolled and her chest tightened. She had to give him what he needed too. "Crone, I never blamed you for my grandmother's death, but if it will release you from your burden… I forgive you," she whispered. His body visibly relaxed.

"Thank you." He held out his hand. "It's time to meet the others."

She nodded, wondering how one minute she could experience a mind-blowing orgasm and the next feel so empty. *But this is what you wanted. Crone can give you everything. Freedom and power.* But there was this nagging question.

"Wait!" She'd started to reach for him then hesitated.

"What is it?"

How could she ask this? "Why have you decided to do this? Break the bond?" To the point was always the best.

He leaned in and kissed her cheek. "Because your happiness will always come first." He grabbed her hand and flashed them to the temple. Crone had explained earlier that the holy place had been built in the center of their world. Surrounding it were the seven houses as the Jinn called them, but they were actually small countries. Some bordered by mountains, others by water, but all equally beautiful. Crone's family ruled four of the seven. Or in this case, Efrain, their father ruled them until his children came of age. Armand had already taken over Revania, and his wife, Makayla ruled Eral. Crone would soon take his rightful place ruling Tujan, and Lazaro would one day lead Agana. Here Tessa thought witch politics could sometimes be confusing. It was another reason--besides her lack of power--she never went to council meetings. She had pretty much washed her hands of her people since they'd turned their backs on her family.

Another reason to gain my power. As an elemental witch, she could force the council to allow her to have a seat. She'd finally have the acceptance and respect of her people. With no family, the other witches were all she had, but they'd never once helped her. As she watched Crone take command of the flurry of people who began to file through the open double doors, she realized she witnessed the Jinn who she'd come to know. The powerful man who let nothing stand in his way. Who took what he wanted. When had he become so... Nothing like the man she'd just experienced on the beach. That Jinn had been gentle. Given her what she needed and asked for nothing in return. Once she learned he'd bonded them, she fully expected he would make demands of her. Her mind raced back to something he'd said earlier.

"Taking your virginity so you can gain your grandmother's power? Not happening. You're going to have to take what you desire."

She nearly smacked herself on the head. What an idiot she was. She'd come with the intent of taking what she wanted and walking away. Doing to Crone exactly what she feared he'd do to her. It was why he refused to take her virginity. He was afraid of becoming too close to her and then losing her. *Take what you desire.* He'd already made it clear he wanted her happiness. If she desired to leave and be free, he'd grant it. If she desired to stay, at least he would know that she wanted him and not what he held.

In an instant, she knew exactly what she wanted. After this was over, she would tell Crone.

CHAPTER TWELVE

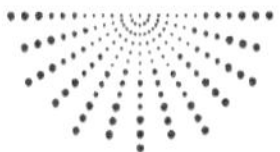

Crone stood at the front of the temple with his brothers and father but kept Tessa in view. He'd positioned her so she was surrounded by their best and strongest, yet he was still on edge. Would be until this nightmare was over and she was safe. Lazaro leaned in.

"She is a beautiful woman, your witch."

Crone's heart weighed heavy. "She isn't mine. I have to let her go."

"Shit, brother. What happened?"

He finally looked away and focused on his sibling. "She needs to be free. If I make her stay then I'm no better than the warlock."

"Damn. Does she know?"

"I told her. She seemed surprised but didn't argue, which I can only assume means she's happy about it." He wasn't. It had taken everything he had to let her go. Hell, in reality he hadn't done so yet and realized the only way to stay away from her was to give up everything. It was his secret that when he gave up Tara's power, he'd also be giving up his own. He'd realized it was the only way he could stay away from Tessa and let her have a life. He'd bargained with the witch who had bonded him that should he require it, she would break it and hand all that he was to Tessa.

"I'm sorry," Lazaro stated. "I really think you wanted to make this work." Before Crone could reply, their father stepped in.

"We are ready." Efrain nodded, and the brothers joined Armand.

The temple was packed. Over three hundred Jinn had crammed inside and another hundred stood outside. They began to summon their power, concentrating on one single person.

Makayla.

In low tones, the chanting echoed across the marble floor and stone walls. Power arched and flashed in various colors until it melted together and began to swirl in the front of the room. Crone had never seen anything like it before. It was simply a thing of beauty as it took on a life of its own and began to form a doorway.

It's working!

Crone glanced at Armand. A look of hope stirred in his brother's eyes that hadn't been there since his wife had gone missing.

The outline of a simple wooden door formed. Its interior still faded in and out, struggling to become solid.

"Keep at it!" Efrain yelled above the chanting.

Crone checked on Tessa. Her eyes were wide with amazement as she stared at the magic floating around the room. Her lips moved and followed the chant even though she didn't know the language spoken. Ancient and rarely used. It was something that came to them naturally; it was so engrained into their DNA.

The door had become solid and now stood wide open. On the other side, the faint form of the queen could be seen. She turned her head and studied them, likely confused by what she saw and not sure if it was a trick. Suddenly her face lit up, and she ran.

"Armand!" Makayla sprinted through the door and into her husband's open arms. The door shut and fizzled out as a thunderous round of applause pierced the night air. Their queen was back.

Crone shoved his way in to hug his sister-in-law. "Damn it woman, don't scare us like that again."

She let out a nervous laugh. "I'm so happy to be home. I can't believe how you all managed that." She slipped back into Armand's arms. No doubt, the Jinn didn't want his wife far from him.

Crone searched for Tessa, but she wasn't where she'd been a minute ago. He made his way through the thicket of people and approached the two females that had been standing next to her.

"Did you see where Tessa went?"

They both looked at him, eyes wide with terror. "She simply vanished," the one replied.

"As soon as the queen ran through, the witch let out a cry and she was gone," stated the other.

Panic crawled across his skin like a thousand scorpions. "What do you mean?"

"By the terrified look on her face, I think she was taken." The girl next to him fidgeted. "I tried to reach for her but was too late."

"Fuck!" Crone spun and searched for his father. "Out of my way," he growled as he shoved the others so he could make his way outside. The air was still charged with too much magic, making it impossible to use his own power to reach the outside faster. He'd have to charge his way through.

Once he finally saw the opening to the outside, he gave one last shove and cleared the entry to the temple. Outside was still crowded, but at least his magic worked and he could summon his father.

A biting grip had grabbed Tessa, its talons sliding into her skin and muscle. She'd tried to scream, but only a whimper came forth. Seconds later, she found herself whisked away from the Jinn surrounding her and shoved into a dark, stinky cell. *What the hell happened?*

"I'll tell you what happened."

Oh hell. She'd recognize Zadicus' voice anywhere.

"When those stupid Jinn opened the portal, I took advantage. The power of black magic is far superior."

Tessa ran to the bars and shook them. "Let me out!" She sensed the magic surrounding her and knew there was no way to escape.

"I'm very disappointed in you." Zadicus moved from the shadows to stand in front of the bars holding her prisoner. "I would have been different than my father and his father. I would have loved you had you given me the chance."

She crossed her arms in an effort to provide some comfort. "You would have bred me like a whore. Last time I checked that wasn't love." No, love was the respect Crone had shown her, and it was something she realized she felt for him also. She had been ready to tell him she wanted to stay and build a life together, but the warlock in front of her had spoiled that chance. For that, she hated him more.

"Yes, I would have had you impregnated by another. It's part of the curse. I'm as bound by it as you are," Zadicus snarled.

She dropped her hands and wrapped her fingers around the bars. "Why don't you break it. We can both go on with our lives." Hope welled. Maybe she could talk some sense into him.

"It isn't that simple, and why would I want to? Now I have to find a way to break your bond with the Jinn so you can bear a daughter."

"What the hell do you mean it's not that simple?" Hope had been replaced with rage. "Break the stupid curse then you can marry and have your own damn children. Leave mine out of it."

He simply shook his head and walked away.

"Come back here!" she shouted, but he ignored her and disappeared into the shadows. Tessa growled and shook the bars as if they would miraculously open and set her free. There had to be a way out. Certainly, Crone would find her. After all, he'd done so before. "But he may think I left on my own." She'd not said anything to him that would lead him to believe she wanted him for anything other than her grandmother's power. Hell, she wasn't even sure herself when she'd finally come to the realization that he was more than that to her. Tessa stepped away from the bars and focused on her surroundings. If she wanted to get out of this mess, she'd have to rescue herself. She'd be damned if she'd go down without a fight.

❧

Crone was nearly insane with panic when his father finally arrived by his side.

"I'm sorry I was delayed. I had to make sure my daughter was okay," Efrain stated before his brows shot downward. "What's the matter?"

"He took Tessa. Somehow, when we had the doorway open for Kayla to come back..." Crone fisted his hands. "He fucking took her."

His father stiffened. "You're sure of this?" He looked around. "She didn't simply wander off?"

"No. I spoke with the women near her. They said she vanished." He had a hard time standing still long enough to explain. Old memories of death and destruction surfaced. The killing machine that he'd once been had come to life, and that man was willing to destroy anything and everyone who stood in his path.

"Deep breath, son. We need to keep a level head if we're to find her." He touched Crone's shoulder.

"That's the problem. I can't breathe. I thought I could let her go, but I was mistaken. That witch has gotten under my skin." When had he realized he loved her? It seemed impossible, but he wanted her more than he'd ever wanted anything, and he was willing to do whatever it took to find her and make her see things his way.

Efrain shook his head. "Do my son's ever listen to me? Why you always think you can fight what destiny has set before you is beyond me. Armand thought he could walk away too, but look how happy he is now that he realized his error. Your youngest brother... That's another story." Before Crone could reply, his father had whisked him away and back to his study.

"What are we doing here?" He needed to be doing something, yet he had no idea where to begin. His father stared at him as if he were daft.

"You need to give your witch some credit. I'm sure she'll manage her way back home." Efrain shuffled some papers on his desk. "In the meantime. War has been declared on the warlock nation. Namely the Demois clan. We will seek out and destroy every last one of them. This kidnapping of my daughters will not go unpunished."

Crone closed his eyes and inhaled, seeking peace. "Your daughters? And by the way, Tessa may be a witch, but her power is not her own. The woman is one hot mess." *And she's my hot mess.* He didn't care if she turned the house into a barnyard. He gladly let her.

"Yes, my daughters, since I fully expect Tessa to become part of the family. You underestimate her."

Crone sensed his father was hiding something. "What are you not telling me?"

The elder Jinn smiled. "You always could read between the lines. When I spent that short amount of time with Tessa, I gave her power a boost."

His father never ceased to amaze him. "She never mentioned it."

"She doesn't know, but she'll discover it when she looks."

Crone blinked. With his patience wearing thin, he needed to tread lightly or his father would remind him in a most painful way how he was still the stronger Jinn. "Father. This is my mate we're talking about and for the love of everything sacred..."

Efrain held his hand up. "I was mated once and I haven't forgotten what it feels like."

"Of course, forgive me, but certainly you realize my need to rip something to shreds." Crone sometimes forgot how it must be for his father being alone. His mother had passed several years ago. "Perhaps it's time you found some companionship."

"Don't worry about me. On to your mate. She will find the little boost I gave her, I have every faith. In the meantime, I have friends who reside on the witch's council. We'll go before them and ask for help in locating Zadicus." The elder waved his hand over the desk and a map appeared. A rush of relief came over Crone, and he wanted to hug his father, but that would have to wait until he had Tessa back in his arms.

The map shimmered and a dot of yellow appeared. "The council resides here." Efrain pointed.

Crone studied the mountainous region. "I know that area, but had no idea the council was there."

"They stay well hidden when they reside there. Lucky for us, this is the time of year they are in session."

"So what do we do? Simply waltz in there and hope they will see us?" He didn't wish to doubt his father, but everything was riding on this.

"That is exactly what we are going to do. In the meantime, I have our best men standing by. Armand wanted to join us, but I knew you'd insist he stay with Kayla, and Lazaro... he went hunting for Ares," Efrain stated.

"While I'm curious why he's looking for the cat, I'm anxious to begin the search for my mate."

His father snapped his fingers, and the map faded away. "Then let's go."

CHAPTER THIRTEEN

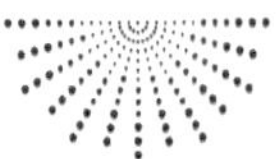

essa dug deep and summoned her inner strength, determined to at least try to make an escape. It was all she could do not to let her attitude sour. After all, she'd never had much luck getting her magic to cooperate. *No, don't think like that. This will work!* She stopped in front of the bars, wrapped her fingers around the metal, and closed her eyes. She envisioned the bars softening like butter, bending enough to allow her to walk between them. The metal began to warm in her hands and she tried hard to keep her positive attitude. When she opened her eyes, she nearly jumped back.

"Oh my hell!" She'd done it. For once in her life, she had accomplished exactly what she'd set out to do. "Okay, Tessa don't get cocky." She still had to escape without detection. Slipping between the bent metal, she stepped into the dank corridor. From what she could gather, she was either deep inside a mountain or underground. Either way, it would be treacherous.

She kept to the stone wall and followed the pathway upward but stopped several feet away from her cell. "Cripes, what an idiot I am." She was so used to her magic disobeying her, she didn't even think to try casting a spell to open a portal. Pulling in a deep breath, she quietly chanted but nothing happened.

Shit.

Okay, so back to working her way out on foot. Maybe Zadicus magic was blocking her. It did take a lot more power to cast a portal than bending some bars. When she got out in the open, she'd try again. In the meantime, she continued to follow the path, slipping once on the wet surface and nearly falling to her knees. Her skin pimpled from the cold, and she wished for something warmer.

"Son of a..." She stroked the soft sleeves of a fuzzy black sweater that had wrapped itself around her. "I need to be careful what I wish for, but I do wish to get out of here in one piece." She waited. "Yeah, figures my power would be fickle." Still, she had to wonder what had happened to suddenly make things go her way. Could Crone have something to do with it? Damn, but she was desperate to find her way back to him, so she could tell him that she wanted him. She only hoped he still desired her.

She'd been so in awe of her new outerwear that she hadn't noticed the voices until she was almost upon them. Coming to an abrupt halt, she saw a dim light flicker ahead and panic gripped her. Again she tried to summon a portal but was greeted with only failure. She chewed her lip and racked her brain on what to do. Going back was not an option, so she tiptoed forward closer to the light, until she was able to peer around the corner.

Zadicus.

"Khrom, our top priority is to find a way to reverse this bond between the Jinn and my witch," the warlock spoke.

His witch? Ass.

"Master, it would seem the most logical would be to kill the Jinn."

"Revenge will be mine for what he did to my grandfather. Making Crone suffer will prove more sport than simply killing him." Zadicus walked to a shelf and began pulling down bottles. "Making Tessa watch while I destroy Crone and his family should be sufficient punishment for involving them in the first place."

Bile rose and scratched her throat raw. She was responsible for this entire mess. Already the queen had been abducted, but luckily she'd returned. How long, though, before Zadicus was able to carry out his threats. If she gave herself up––no that wouldn't solve the fact she was bonded to Crone. Zadicus would still destroy the Jinn simply to torture her. There had to be a way to stop the warlock. Tessa had to hurry and find a way out before they caught her. Even though she had some working magic, she wasn't going to depend on it sticking around.

Crone and his father took a portal to the outskirts of a small village that could only be seen by other immortals. It seemed this was the time of year when others made their way to the witches to barter for favors. As they strode past several demons, a couple of shifters, and an ever-elusive fairy, they were cast evil glares. His father barged up to a long table where an elderly woman sat.

She lifted her gaze. "Back of the line." She pointed.

"I am Efrain, ruler of the houses of Agana and Tujan."

The witch raised a thick brow. "Who is he?" She jerked her head toward Crone.

His father grinned. "That is my son, Crone. Soon to be ruler of the house of Tujan."

Her mouth gaped. "The Crone of legends?"

Efrain's smile widened. "The one and only."

The woman jumped from her seat, turning to a guard who stood at the gate. "Let them in and make sure they are escorted directly to the council." The man nodded and pushed open the gate, giving them access. Once on the other side, another guard directed them down a brick path to a large log home. Inside they were led down a set of stairs and to a large room. In the center was a table that stretched several feet, and seven witches, four female and three male, sat around it. The man at the head rose to his feet.

"Efrain, how good to see you. To what do we owe this visit?"

"Hector," Efrain reached for the witch's hand and grasped it in a firm shake. "I've come to beg a favor." He looked to Crone. "This is my son, Crone."

"Yes, we heard he was here." Hector shook Crone's hand then directed them to two vacant chairs. "Please sit. I must say we are honored to have you here."

To say Crone was slightly confused would hardly indicate how he felt. "I'm touched but not sure how I've commanded such an honor."

The witch settled back into his seat. "Your skill at slaying warlocks is legendary."

Of course they would have heard of him. Morden had several warlocks killed during Crone's enslavement. There was no love lost between most any species and the warlock's, but especially the witches. Most witches were peaceable and one with the earth. Warlocks were the epitome of evil.

"You must also know that several witches lost their lives during that time," Crone stated. While it wasn't many, he'd still committed a crime against Hector's people.

Hector steepled his fingers. "Of course we were distressed over their deaths, but for what it's worth, you showed mercy in your killing of our people. It was that action that led us to investigate, and we discovered you were not acting of your own free will."

Crone didn't have time for the guilt he felt. He wanted Tessa back. Now. "I am truly sorry. I went into the agreement knowing full well what was expected of me."

The witch's green eyes sparked. "True, and I don't doubt you've lived with the guilt of your actions. I might also add--to ease your mind--that those who fell by your hand were criminals. Had they been caught by us, they would have met a similar fate."

That did help. Some.

Crone looked to his father then to each individual at the table. "If there is any punishment I must face then so be it. However, first I need your help to find my mate. She is a wi—"

"We are aware Tessa is your mate," a woman across from him spoke. "Tara's request to the ancestors was heard by the council."

Suddenly Crone grew angry. "Why have the witch's done nothing to help Tessa?"

Another female leaned forward. "We cannot fight the curse or the warlocks. It has pained us that we've not been able to protect our own. Unfortunately, the Blackwood women have paid the price. Tara must have realized, when she met you, that you could help Tessa finally break her family's curse."

He curled his fingers into a fist and slammed them on the table. He should be angry that Tara basically used him for her own agenda, but that's not what pissed him off. "Help me find my mate." He didn't care how or why Tessa had come to be his. He only knew she did, and that was all that mattered.

Hector nodded. "We have spies who know where Zadicus hides. We can get you in, but Tessa has to be the one to end the warlock."

It made sense. "I have two of the three items she needs to break the curse."

"I'm afraid you've run out of time for that. You'll have to take her virginity and give back her grandmother's power, along with sharing some of your own," another female stated.

"What the hell? So I'm expected to sweep in there and fuck my mate before Zadicus discovers us?" Several of the females turned bright red. Well, they deserved to blush for even thinking that he should treat Tessa in such a manner.

"Umm. You only need to take her virginity. How you do it is totally up to you," she replied.

"Can't I simply kill the bastard?" That was more his style anyway, plus he wanted Tessa's first time to be special. Not something that was taken in the middle of a war zone.

"I'm afraid the warlock has been busy spreading his seed. We've no idea how many sons he has at the moment, but if this curse isn't broken, it will affect your daughters." Hector was matter of fact.

Crone's head spun, so many emotions boiled and were ready to erupt like a toxic volcano. The world would end if anyone touched his children. "I will do what is required," he snarled. "Lead the way."

❦

Tessa tiptoed past the open doorway, her heart ready to leap from her chest; she was so fearful of getting caught. When she looked over her shoulder to make sure she wasn't being followed, she ran into a wall. When she looked back, she tipped her head to meet the dark blue gaze of the most gorgeous man in the world. She started to whisper his name when he placed his finger over her lips and shook his head. She understood and would ask questions later, after she kissed the hell out of him. Before she knew what was happening, he wrapped his strong arms around her and the scenery began to melt away. In the distance, she swore she heard the faint screams of pain along with a tinge of smoke.

Seconds later they were back on the beach that was beginning to feel more like home. Waves crashed on the sand as the sun began to show itself on the horizon. Brilliant colors mottled the sky, but her attention was on the man standing in front of her.

He pulled his shirt over his head and tossed it to the ground.

She gulped and savored the view.

"Tessa. It's a long story, but your people say you have to break the curse. Before we begin, I need to make a few things clear."

She licked her lips. Were they really going to have sex? "Okay."

"How you lose your virginity is up to you. Remember *mi amor*, whatever you desire, it's yours to take." He snapped his fingers and a large carpet, woven in vibrant colors appeared on the sand. Half a dozen pillows were laid out at one end.

"Umm, what if Zadicus shows up?" God, just looking at him and the thought of what they were about to do had heat pooling in her sex.

"My people have him detained." He stepped closer. "He will have to die."

"I know." She understood what would be required of her.

He placed his hands on her shoulders. "I want one thing made very clear before we begin."

"Yes?"

"I can't let you go. I know I promised but…" He lifted his hand and slid his fingers into her hair. "I need you, Tessa, and I will spend the rest of my life making you happy. Just please say you'll give us a chance." He traced his thumb across her bottom lip.

She nearly melted, parted her lips, and nipped his thumb. "I wanted to tell you, before everything happened, that I choose you. I want us to be together, and I was foolish thinking I could fight fate."

He leaned closer, his lips only inches away from hers. "I'm so happy to hear that. Now tell me, what do you want?" he whispered. "I need to hear the words." His lids were heavy and his eyes burned with desire.

Her own need grew until she thought she'd burst. "You. I want you to make love to me. Do we have time for that?"

He grinned. "I will always make time for you, *mi amor*." He touched his lips to hers and she opened. Met his tongue and matched every swipe while reaching for the button on his jeans. She wanted him naked. He broke free, and she groaned in despair.

"I need you naked, but as desperate as I am with need for you, I want to do this the old-fashioned way." He moved his hands to her hips and slipped them under her tee. Lifting the fabric as he slid along her skin until he was to her breasts. Her excitement grew with the knowledge he was going to undress her rather than use his magic to make her clothes disappear.

He continued pulling the tee over her head until it was free from her body then tossed it to the ground. Next, he bent and kissed between her breasts, his facial hair soft on her skin. Her nipples hardened in anticipation, begging for his attention. He licked and nipped along the edge of her bra, teasing. She tipped her head back to allow better access, and he kissed his way up her neck while his hands found the clasp and unhooked it. Before she realized it, that too had landed on the ground, and her breasts pressed against his warm skin. He stepped back and his gaze roamed from hers, downward, and landed on her chest. He licked his lips and looked as if he wanted to devour her.

Before she could make a move, he grabbed her and laid her on the carpet, pillows cushioning her head.

"You are perfect." He swirled his tongue over a nipple then sucked it into his mouth.

She moaned and arched into him, her fingers clutching the rug's fabric. He lifted his head, an evil grin on his lips.

"You like?"

"Mmm, most definitely."

His grin growing wider, he licked his way down her belly. He stopped to trace a circle around her belly button while he unsnapped her jeans. With a quick jerk, he had them removed along with her undies.

"Such beauty. I am humbled." He kissed her calf, working his way up her thigh and along her hip, before he ran his tongue across her pelvic bone and to her other hip where he repeated the process in reverse.

Tessa trembled with anticipation, her core burning with liquid heat. "I can't take much more," she whispered. "Please, make love to me."

"You're not ready. Soon." He dived between her legs. His hot breath made her clit throb, so she slid her fingers into his hair to encourage him. He took the hint and licked between her folds.

"Ohh." Damn, the things she'd been missing out on. Then again, she couldn't think of anyone else she'd rather have introduce her to the wonders of sex.

CHAPTER FOURTEEN

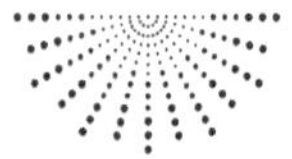

*C*rone wanted to drown in Tessa's essence, her intoxicating scent. He had to fight to keep control of the reins. This was her first... No, he was her first, and he had to admit his ego was on overdrive.

He inhaled. Took another swipe through her folds before he swirled around her clit.

She arched into him, a hiss escaping her lips.

He was going to enjoy the hell out of her coming, until she begged for him to stop. He pinned her hips to the ground and slipped his tongue into her channel. Her hips gyrated and her nails dug into his scalp. Rough was how he liked to play, but this time he'd let her see his softer side. Later they would have more time to explore each other, and he could hardly wait.

Increasing the speed of his thrusts, he peered over her belly and watched her lids close, her lips part. Damn, she was beautiful. He wanted to watch her come, so he moved to her clit and sucked.

She exploded.

Before she could even catch her breath, he gently inserted a finger, and using a twisting motion, he worked at stretching her. She gasped.

"Damn that's good, but I want to feel you inside of me. I need you so bad," she whispered.

"Soon, I need to make sure you're good and wet for me." Inserting a second finger, he pumped a little faster until he sensed her on the edge. He sucked on her clit and rolled his tongue across it until she came in shuddering waves. Now she was ready, and thank god, because he couldn't wait another second to seat himself deep inside her.

He pushed himself up and kissed his way up her belly, poised between her legs. "Are you sure?"

She ran her fingertips across his chest. "Yes."

He fisted his cock and rubbed the head along her folds, spreading her juices and hissing at the heat of her against him. The woman was on fire and he pressed the tip until he'd entered. "Let me know if I hurt you. That's the last thing I want to do," he spoke through his clenched teeth, reminding himself he needed to practice restraint.

"It doesn't hurt."

He pushed further, going slow to allow her time to adjust. He bent his head, sucked a nipple into his mouth, and circled his tongue around, causing her to lift her hips and take more of him. He liked that, and it gave him an idea. "I'm going to roll us so you can be on top and take me at your own pace."

"I like that idea."

He slipped his hand under her waist and with ease rolled to his back, careful not to slip any deeper inside her. "I rather like you on top." He reached up and rolled her nipples between his fingers. Her head tipped back, and she took more of him. Inch by tight wet inch, she slid down his shaft until he thought he'd blow a nut. Being inside her was heaven. It felt right in so many ways.

Tessa dug her fingers into his chest, her parted lips red and full, and dropped her chin until their gazes met. Her brown eyes darkened with desire and she slid home. Her hot sheath wrapped around him like a velvet glove, and she grinned. "Damn you feel good. I like sex."

Oh, this witch was the perfect mate for him. He wanted to grip her hips and fuck the hell out of her, but he held steady. "You can have sex with me anytime you wish," were the only words he could manage.

"Anytime?" She raised herself until only the tip of his cock remained inside her warmth.

He moved his thumb to rest on her clit and enjoyed the look on her face. "Anytime. Several times a day if you desire."

"Oh I like that idea." She slid back down, taking him to his balls and began a steady pace of pumping his shaft. "Christ, I'm gonna come again."

He massaged her nub and could feel her tightening around him. He wouldn't last much longer. "Come for me, baby."

She gripped his chest and squeezed his cock as her orgasm took her, and she yelled out. Her spasms milked him, and his balls pulled tight as jets of semen shot up his cock. He grabbed her hips and held her tight to him while his own orgasm continued to rack his body. When finally they were able to catch their breath, she laid her head on his chest, and he wrapped his arms around her.

"I want to stay like this forever," her voice barely audible over the crashing waves.

He swallowed. There were so many things they had to discuss. Everything had happened so fast. "We can live here if you want." He stroked her hair. "Any place you want to go."

She raised her head and looked at him. "I guess we have a lot of decisions to make."

Should she start by confessing her feelings? Then there was... "Oh my god!"

Crone's eyes widened with concern. "What? What's the matter?"

"Nana's power. I can feel it." She pushed herself up to sitting, the friction of his still hard cock causing her to moan.

He smiled. "Of course you can."

She planted her hands on his chest. Firm muscle bunched under her fingers. "I have to admit, I forgot all about it." She dropped her gaze to his lips. "I kinda got caught in the moment."

"I gave it back to you." He reached up and cupped her face. "When we connected, it surfaced. I'd never felt it before, but I could tell instantly that I held a power different from my own. I simply fed it back to you."

"Wow. I feel like I've been recharged." In more ways than one. There was so much power zinging through her, she feared short-circuiting.

"What of the curse?" he inquired.

"Right." She lifted herself and rolled off, missing him already. "I need to perform the ritual." She noted the sun was now midway in the sky. While the moon made a witch more powerful, she dared not wait until later. Zadicus would know her virginity was gone, and he would come. Of that she had no doubt. Jumping to her feet, she was fully clothed before she even realized it.

"Oh. Did you do that?" Crone was also on his feet and dressed. Damn it.

"No. You dressed yourself. I can feel your magic and it's glorious." He stepped beside her. "What now?"

"I need to use the elements to break the curse, and quickly, before Zadicus shows up." Tessa held out her hand and produced a stick. No longer surprised her magic worked, she was more confident than ever and having Crone by her side only increased it. She began to draw a circle in the sand and once complete she took a second look to make sure it was complete and they were standing inside it.

"Now, I need you to stand behind me and put your hands on my waist. I need your help to channel all this energy."

"Like a familiar?" He moved behind her and she felt the warmth of his hands through her top.

"Yes. I'm not sure why, but something tells me you'll be able to help me in the same way." She faced so the sun was to their backs, and she was looking down a lone stretch of beach.

"I am your mate. It would be common for me to balance your

power." He kissed the top of her head. She supposed he was correct, and it made perfect sense.

"Okay, I'm going to begin the chant." She stretched her arms in front of her, palms upward.

"*Doetncu graessum, iusuid, nonuiscri, quitebi, iber, ueffeci, proplemi, haechaecui.*"

The wind picked up speed. "*Undepami. Quaeci sacoquammo, fuiinone coaquibus, ibiliud.*"

Clouds raced across the sky and she was one with Mother Earth. Her magic welled from some place deep within her. She felt Crone guide her, helping to channel and keep control as her magic grew more powerful.

"*Nepolios quasuna, mideipu, postquiaixi, quafonon, eiussatum, innorat etcum, ergara. Rocuite fasuneum, saeota, acetia, sicpofa, uequammeum.*"

The sky darkened and the waves beat angrily on the beach.

"You can never break the curse!" Zadicus was in front of her, screaming obscenities. She felt Crone stir. *No! Do not break our bond.* Hell's bells, she'd just entered his mind and spoken to him.

"How much longer?" he whispered in her ear.

Not much.

"*Undepami. Quaeci sacoquammo, fuiinone coaquibus, ibiliud.Undepami. Quaeci sacoquammo, fuiinone coaquibus, ibiliud.*"

Power surged from the warlock, but she held steady and Crone helped her keep focus. Almost done, she prayed to the ancestors the next step happened fast, so she could finish the spell. Then it did.

An ominous cloud covered the sun, and the sky went black. Seconds later, the full moon hung overhead.

"Son of a bitch," Crone growled behind her. She had just turned day into night. Now to finish.

"*Etuae anoueniquam, taestquem, ueestiam, copostni, quiciuigetas, deeto, oquodcauit.*"

Lightning streaked across the sky accompanied by a thunderous boom. The wind whipped flames around her circle. Current flowed down her arms and exited her fingertips in a jolt so powerful, she would have fallen backward if not for Crone. Her power made a direct hit. Zadicus screamed as the fire grew higher then everything fell silent. The fire was gone, the waves a bare whisper, and the sun began to shine as the grey clouds broke up.

"I did it!" She spun to face Crone. The full force of the sun now shone down on them.

"Damn. You are one helluva witch. I've heard of Elementals, but never have I seen one in action. Remind me not to piss you off." He smiled.

"I couldn't have done it alone." She touched his lips with her finger. "You truly are my other half, and somewhere along this crazy journey you stole my heart. I love you." His body relaxed.

"Does this mean you're staying?"

"Of course. That is if you'll still have me." She hoped she hadn't just scared the hell out of him.

"You can't get rid of me that easy." He pulled her to his chest. "The moment I kissed you on this beach I knew I loved you. My stubborn self just didn't want to admit it right away."

She laughed.

"Did you destroy Zadicus?"

She kissed his naked chest. "Yes, and I took his power. The curse is broken, and his children will never be a threat again."

"How can you be sure?" He gripped her hair and gently pulled her head back so she had to look at him.

"The ancestors whispered in my ear only moments before Zadicus vanished. I did it, Crone. Our daughters will never have to bear the curse." She licked her lips. "That is if you want children."

"Several and I'm ready to start now."

Crone couldn't be more proud of Tessa and how she managed to handle her magic, as if it had been a part of her all her life. He was also proud to be her familiar. It had been amazing to connect with her, feel her power, and help channel it right where she'd needed it. The woman would be a force to be reckoned with.

She gave him a wicked grin. "That witch? The one who bonded you?"

"Yes?"

"Remind me to thank her. Do you think your father would perform my bonding?"

"He would be honored." It was customary when *vetembas* were of another species that an elder perform the bonding. Crone had already fulfilled his end when he sought the witch. Now, Tessa wanted to complete it using his father. "But are you sure? Take time to be certain." Once she completed the bond, there would be no going back.

"I couldn't be more certain. Nana knew what she was doing by bringing us together. I wish I could have known her."

"She and your mother are very proud," Hector spoke from behind. Crone turned and the entire witch council stood on the sand. Hector moved forward.

"We have come to tell you how sorry we are that we were never able to help your family." He cleared his throat. "The Demois clan was very powerful."

Crone watched as Tessa stepped closer; tears threatened her. "I thought you didn't care," she sniffed.

One of the females stepped forward. "We always cared and never stopped looking for a way to fight. We wanted to tell you but feared what they might do to the council. We had to keep a low profile."

Tessa nodded. "I understand."

"You will take your place as head council member now?" Hector asked.

"I'd be honored." She whirled to face Crone. "I want to perform the bond here, in the place I hold most dear, this beach. My people are here." She stepped into him. "I never thought I would be this happy. Can we?"

"Your wish is my command." He snapped his fingers. Several carpets blanketed the sand and his family stood by smiling. Efrain approached.

"Are you ready, daughter?"

"Oh, let me change." She went from jeans to a white gown, her hair cascading around her shoulders in curls just how he loved it. Crone followed suit and changed into a black tux.

"Does this please you?"

She looked as if she wanted to devour him. "It does." She turned to Efrain. "Can we hurry?"

He chuckled. "Kneel, facing each other." He produced a wide, gold strip of cloth. Crone laced his fingers in Tessa's, and his father wound the ribbon around their hands, binding them together.

The elder Jinn chanted in their ancient language, sprinkling gold dust over their heads, and it was done. Their bond was complete, never to be broken. Two nations now brought together.

"Crone, son of Efrain. Ruler of the house of Tujan. May you and your queen enjoy an eternity of love and be blessed with many children," Efrain shouted and the crowd roared.

His new bride looked at him. "Ruler?"

A surprise to him as well. "A gift from my father."

The corner of her lip curled. "Well, my king. Take me home and let's get started on those children."

He pulled her into his arms. "My little witch. I intend to do just that."

ABOUT THE AUTHOR

Award winning and bestselling author Valerie Twombly grew up watching Dark Shadows over her mother's shoulder, and from there her love of the fanged creatures blossomed. Today, Valerie has decided to take her darker, sensual side and put it to paper. When she is not busy creating a world full of steamy, hot men and strong, seductive women, she juggles her time between a full-time job, hubby and her two German shepherd dogs, in Northern IL. Valerie is a member of Romance Writers of America and Fantasy, Futuristic and Paranormal Romance Writers. She is also the founder of the Sexy Scribblers. A group of romance writers who get together and write free stories for their fans.

Sign up for Valerie's newsletter and be the first to hear about new releases, receive special excerpts and exclusive contests. http://valerietwombly.com/newsletter-sign/

Follow Valerie
www.valerietwombly.com

ALSO BY VALERIE TWOMBLY

THE ETERNALLY MATED SERIES

Fall into Darkness: 2nd place: THE ANCIENT CITY ROMANCE AUTHORS'
2016 HEART OF EXCELLENCE READERS' CHOICE AWARDS
&
Finalist: Heart of Denver Romance Writer's Aspen Gold Contest

Find more Valerie Twombly books at http://valerietwombly.com
Where your supernatural seduction begins

A JINN'S SEDUCTION SERIES

Spanish Nights: Winner of Best Short Fantasy, Preditors & Editors

Find more Valerie Twombly books at http://valerietwombly.com
Where your supernatural seduction begins

An Angel's Torment (Eternally Mated Prequel)

Veiled In Darkness (Eternally Mated #2)

Fall Into Darkness (Eternally Mated #1)

Bound By Darkness (Eternally Mated Novel)

Surrender To Darkness (Eternally Mated Novel)

Unleash The Darkness (Eternally Mated Novella)

Eternal Flame (Guardians #1)

Fatal Desire (Guardians #2)

Primal Hunger (Guardians #3)

Divine Passion (Guardians #3.5)

Amazon Heat (Demon Heat #1)

Emerald Fire (Demon Heat #2)

Spanish Nights, A Jinn's Seduction

Sultry Nights, A Jinn's Seduction

Taken By Desire (Demonic Desires #1)

His Burning Desire (Sparks Of Desire)

Passion Awakened (Beyond The Mist)